THE LAST PLEA

By
ROBERT BLOCH

ARMCHAIR FICTION
PO Box 4369, Medford, Oregon   97501-0168

SO YOU WANT TO BE A ROCK N' ROLL STAR

All Luther Snodgrass wanted was to play his git-tar and make people happy with his music. The problem was that Luther had absolutely no talent—none whatsoever. So it seemed kind of strange that a well-known talent agent like Judge Harmer would take him under his wing. But there was more to Judge Harmer than met the eye. And the contract Luther signed was written in something more than ink.

Join master horror and sci-fi storyteller Robert Bloch, as he spins a delightful fantasy-farce about the long and winding road to the top of the Rock and Roll business. A road that is filled with perverse hilarity and has you walking hand-in-hand with the devil himself…

FOR A COMPLETE SECOND NOVEL, TURN TO PAGE 69

CAST OF CHARACTERS

LUTHER SNODGRASS
This southern country-bumpkin was about as talent-less as they come. So how did he end becoming a pop-music phenom?

JUDGE HARMER
He was the Colonel Parker of the Satanic world, able to take any no-talent loser and make him the world's next Rock n' Roll icon.

MARY JANE HAWKINS
She was beautiful, she was talented—and she hated everything there was about propped up singing stars like Luther Snodgrass.

MOTHER
This retired witch's job was to rid Luther of his oafish southern drawl and turn him into a hip-sounding pop star!

JEFFERSON DAVIS FINK
Finkola was the brew he concocted and sold to an unsuspecting world. It could cure…well…just about anything!

MEDIUM DUNN
He owned a spiritualist parlor in Southern California—and he was Luther's one and only hope of ridding himself of the Devil.

EDDIE PUSS
He helped turn Luther Snodgrass into a top-notch songwriter of the most banal kind of pop-musical schlock.

CHAPTER ONE

THERE was nothing supernatural about the way Clay Clinton got his start.

That part comes later.

In the beginning, there was only Luther Snodgrass, of Crump Creek, Texas.

Nobody paid much attention to Luther Snodgrass at first, including his own mother. She took one look at the squalling brat when he was born, then dumped him in the railway ditch next to the water tower. Within five hours she took the next freight out of town and vanished into Oblivion (Okla.).

All she bequeathed the infant was his name, scribbled with the stub end of a pencil on the inside of a Sterno label. She christened him with a note pinned to half a pair of panties that she ripped down the middle and wound around his spindle-shanks as he lay cradled in an old orange-crate.

Her message was brief and to the point, if any.

To Whoom It may Consern:
Pleese somebody take care of my babey boy his name is Luther Snodgrass after his father the no good sunabich he run out on me in Waco.
Hoping You Are The Same,
—Joyleen Crutt

A gaudy dancer named Hank Peavey found Luther—and his letter of introduction to a waiting world—within a matter of minutes after the freight pulled out. He called the sheriff and the sheriff took the baby to the County Hospital, and the County Hospital (after a few desultory efforts to locate either Joyleen Crutt or the no good sunabich she had honored with the paternity of her offspring) passed the infant on to the County Orphanage at Crump Creek.

Luther Snodgrass did a lot of howling when he was a baby, but nobody can lay credit to discovering him then.

In due time he grew up to attend grammar school, where he pledged allegiance to the American flag, broke three windows, learned how to read *(Goofball Comics)* and write *("Old Ladey Krantz Has Dirtey Penis")* and do elementary sums *("Cigarettes—28¢. Muscatel—59¢ a fifth").*

At the age of sixteen he completed his formal education and his informal education simultaneously—the latter through the kind offices of a young lady named Luletta Switzel. Unfortunately for Luther Snodgrass, Miss Switzel was her father's pride and joy; rivaled in his affections only by the 12-gauge shotgun that he subsequently pointed in Luther's direction.

Luther got out of range in a manner apparently traditional to his family; he hopped the next rattler.

What he did in El Paso we'll probably never know. What he did in Fort Worth was thirty days for vagrancy.

DURING THE next two years it almost seemed as if the young man were destined to become a writer. At least he underwent what is apparently the customary apprenticeship for that career—he was a dishwasher in a restaurant, a house-to-house salesman, a fry-cook, and a merchant seaman. Actually, however, he flunked out on this last requirement. Luther Snodgrass never really went to sea; he merely did some work as an itinerant stevedore on the banana boats moored at the docks in New Orleans.

It was there, presumably, that he picked up his talent for the guitar (along with something else, which he was fortunately able to get rid of after a few visits to the Public Health Clinic). But the musical affliction persisted; probably some of the local roustabouts encouraged him. He even managed to obtain possession of his own instrument—fortunately, nobody asked to examine the dice during the game—and before long he was playing and passing the hat in the French Quarter. The Vieux Carre Association takes a dim view of such activities on Bourbon Street, but he managed to get into a few dives on Decauter and Chartres. He developed a popular repertoire, including such authentic folk classics as *The Harlot of Jerusalem, Christopher Columbo,* and that plaintive ballad, *The Ring-Dang-Doo.*

The few connoisseurs of folk music who heard him agreed unanimously that Josh White in his prime had never sounded anything like that. Luther Snodgrass was already beginning to develop his distinctive wriggling style; he learned that it was better to writhe and keep moving so as to avoid any missiles aimed his way by listeners who *didn't* appreciate his talent.

It was during this period that Opportunity knocked on young Luther's door. That chance of a lifetime appeared.

To be exact, it wasn't really *his* door, but that of Miss Evangeline LaTour, who resided in the Quarter as a young art student (the art being pick-pocketing and the old badger game). And it wasn't really Opportunity knocking, but a gentleman named Jefferson Davis Fink, renowned throughout the sunny Southland as the progenitor, proprietor and sole purveyor of *Finkola.*

WHO HAS not heard of *Finkola*—that antidote for asthma, banisher of bunions, cure for catarrh, destroyer of dandruff, eradicator of eczema; indeed, of all the alphabetically arranged ailments the flesh is heir to, including such obscure sub-Masonian-and-Dixonian-Line afflictions as the running trots, the galloping consumption and the creeping miseries?

If there are any amongst you who remain in ignorance of this amazing new scientific discovery, it is not because of any failing on the part of Jefferson Davis Fink. He has spared neither pain nor expense in his effort to spread the glad tidings of *Finkola's* miraculous healing properties throughout the length and breadth of Dixie. Wherever five watts join together in the conspiracy known as a southern radio station, the *Finkola* jingles jangle forth. Wherever a tall pine or a majestic cypress looms along the highway, a *Finkola* billboard obscures it. Wherever the sweet scent of magnolias mingles upon the soft and balmy breeze, it mingles with the joyfully-drawn breath of a *Finkola* user *(3?% alcohol, by volume).*

"Yeass, honey-chile," said Jefferson Davis Fink to Miss Evangeline LaTour, as he skillfully diverted her caressing fingertips from the neighborhood of his watch-chain. "Ah reckon they ain't hardly nobody nohow who don't guzzle the stuff."

"My aunt Minnie, she used it for a poultice, time she had them boils," Miss LaTour volunteered, eyeing her companions gen-oo-ine 5-carat (slightly yellowish) diamond ring.

"Sure, sugah," Mr. Fink agreed. "It cures most anything, up to *and* including mastitis. And I hear tell it makes a mighty refresh in' douche, too. *Mighty* refresh-in'." Then, "Great bolls o' cotton, what's *that?*"

THAT PROVED to be Luther Snodgrass, returning unexpectedly early from his nightly rounds and roundelays. The sight of the tall, gangling youth, who confronted them menacingly, armed with a guitar, served to both annoy and affright Miss LaTour.

"Ah dam'," she exclaimed, with girlish petulance. "Ah *tole* you to knock, afore you come bargin' in heah thataway."

"Who is this?" inquired Jefferson Davis Fink, sitting up and reaching for his vest.

"Mah *nevvoo,*" Miss LaTour explained. "He's like mah *proto jay.*"

"*Proto jay?* What—all is he a *proto jay* of?"

"Well, he plays *gittar.* Ah been soht of boa' din' him heah whilst he studies up on it."

Noting the look of skepticism on Mr. Fink's face, she turned to Luther and waggled a coy cuticle. "You-all play suthin' foe Mistah Fink, hear?"

Luther heard. And Mr. Fink, whether he was thus inclined or not, heard also.

"Purty?" Miss LaTour inquired.

The least that gallantry demanded was a nod. Mr. Fink gave it, and thus precipitated another selection. Luther was all set to launch into a third, when Mr. Fink held up his hand.

The sight of the diamond silenced the young man.

"You right talented, boy," he declared. "Right talented. Evah think of goin' into the show bizness?"

"Show bizness?" Luther's eyes rivaled the diamond. "Ah been aimin' fer it."

Jefferson Davis Fink cleared his throat, or at least a portion thereof which was not occupied by plug tobacco. "Well, reckon you done hit the mark, son. So happens Ah'm readyin' anothuh extravaganza. Yessiree, anothuh big *Finkola* Fun Festival is 'bout ready to hit the road."

"Do tell!" Luther's reply was academic; actually it was scarcely necessary to tell him anything about the famous *Finkola* productions. Every year a truckload of top talent trouped through the turpentine swamps and bayous, and into the big tent swarmed every man, woman and wood-colt who possessed the *Finkola* label which entitled the bearer to admission. It was all part of Mr. Fink's advertising campaign, and he spared no expense in mounting his entertainments; raiding every cultural Mecca from Grossinger's to Las Vegas in his quest for top talent. And now—

"Boy, Ah'm gonna give you a chance. Yesiree, that's *exactly* what Ah'm gonna do! You're gonna work for me!"

"You mean, play mah *git*-tar in the show? How *about* that?"

"Wonderful!" Evangeline LaTour beamed fondly on Luther and still more fondly on Jefferson Davis Fink. "Ah do appreciate this. Truly Ah do."

"Think nothin' of it. Always ready to encuh-ge talent when Ah see it." Mr. Fink patted Miss LaTour on the thigh in a fatherly fashion and turned to Luther Snodgrass. "Repoht to mah office at the factory tomorrow mohn'in'."

"Yes, *suh!*"

"Meanwhile, kindly git to hell out'n heah."

"Yes, *suh!*"

CHAPTER TWO

THUS, AS every biographer knows, Luther Snodgrass made his professional debut for *Finkola* the following week, in the thriving metropolis of Ague, Louisiana.

What every biographer doesn't know—or carefully neglects to mention—is that the young musician laid a bomb.

A liberal swig of *Finkola* has a tendency to deaden the hearing (indeed, there are some authorities who claim that steady indulgence will eventually deaden the indulger to a point where his only further use for *Finkola* will be as embalming fluid) and the good people of Ague had sampled enough of the nostrum before Luther appeared so that they were more or less inured to the actual sound of his singing and playing.

However, their olfactory powers remained acute, and before Luther had finished his first number, several of the spectators were glancing under the wooden seats in an effort to detect the whereabouts of a sick polecat.

Some of the men in the audience considered slipping out quietly and summoning an emergency meeting of the Klan.

Jefferson Davis Fink, astute showman that he was, got the message. And right after the first show, he delivered it to Luther Snodgrass.

"Out, boy," he said. "You finished."

"Finished? But Mistah Fink, suh—"

"Don' you-all *Mistak Fink suh* me, hear? Git!"

"Ah thought Ah sounded purty good out theah tonight."

"Good foh what? Lookee heah, boy, Ah'm sellin' medicine to make folks feel bright an' sassy. Then you come on, a membah of mah own company, an' you sound like a hog with it's ham caught in a bob-wire fence. Call that smart advertisin'? No, son, you gotta go."

"Please, give me anothuh chance."

"Sorry. Powerful sorry."

"But you-all cain't leave me stranded heah. Got no grit-money, got nothin'—"

"Heah." Jefferson Davis Fink held out a five-dollar-bill and a bottle of *Finkola*; "This ought to see you back to town. You-all can drink the bottle on the bus. Compliments of the house."

AND THAT was all Luther Snodgrass could get out of him.

In the end he trudged away, guitar in one hand, grip in the other. But the bus station was closed, and there would be no transportation available until ten o'clock the next morning, so Luther didn't go Greyhound.

He picked at his grits and some iguana gumbo in Ague's sole culinary establishment; meanwhile squandering another fifty cents in the jukebox to play the latest recordings by Elvis Presley, Jerry Lee Lewis and The Platters.

"Ah kin sing evah-bit as good as they," he muttered. "Louder, even!"

The thought—as well as the sounds—understandably depressed him. So much so that after he left the restaurant he spent his remaining capital for a bottle of something called *Old Poontang-A Blend:* *85% Neutral Spirits, 15% Hostile Spirits.* It was something like that, anyway; he didn't bother to read the label. And he didn't bother to delay in consuming the contents. By the time he'd finished, Luther made up his mind to hitchhike back to New Orleans. He took the road to the Crescent City, but it was very dark outside, and somehow he seemed to have missed his way.

The next thing he remembered was wandering down a bayou byway which led deeper and deeper into the swamps. The night was black as pitch and even smelled that way; tarry bubbles oozed from the swamp as Luther trod a path never used even by day, and then only by Voodoo conjure-men. A mist crept out of the trees, and Luther shivered. He emptied the bottle and tossed it away, then stumbled on.

"Ah'm purely lost," he complained, sitting down on an old log and fishing out the other bottle, containing *Finkola.* He uncorked and attacked it, and before long, it was attacking him.

Perhaps the *Finkola* was to blame. I'm not going to attempt to sway your opinion. You'll have to decide for yourself. At any rate, nothing happened to Luther Snodgrass until he began to drink the stuff.

"Lost!" he sighed. "Nowhere, U.S.A.!"

IT SUDDENLY occurred to him that he was addressing his complaints to an exceedingly large alligator, which had crawled up out of the bubbling blackness and was perched on the log beside him.

Luther put his arm around the alligator's neck.

"Whassa matter, ole buddy-buddy?" he asked the saurian. "Y'all look purty green around the gills. What you need is a slurp of *Finkola*." He extended the bottle. "Mebbe it'll help you to git rid o' them warts, too!"

The alligator shook its head politely.

"Party-pooper!" muttered Luther, bitterly. He took another swig. His mood changed. "Ah don't blame you. Nobuddy wants to drink with me. Nobuddy wants to heah me sing an' play. Nobuddy loves me. Ah jus' ain't appreciated, nohow. Why for is evvy-buddy agin us artists?"

The alligator shrugged.

"What's Elvis got that Ah ain't got?" Luther demanded. "How come folks make such a fuss ovah a square piano-player like this heah Albert Schweitzer?"

The alligator started to squirm off the log.

"Don' leave me!" Luther wailed. "Ah craves sympathy. You see befo' you a beat-down cat. Ah's sick of try in' the ha'hd way. A man gits fed up, you know? Right now, Ah'd sell mah soul fo' a little ole hunk of prosperity."

The alligator edged away.

"Git me out'n this swamp," Luther implored, clutching vainly at the departing reptile and falling backwards off the log into the muddy ooze. "Take me to your Leader!"

That's what the man said.

Of course, it was only a current phrase; a commonplace expression, like the one about selling one's soul. And naturally, the alligator was only an alligator.

YOU CAN interpret it that way if you like. On the other hand, you may choose to believe otherwise.

In either case, all I can do is offer the facts in the matter.

Which were, and are, as follows. Luther fell off the log into the mud. When he sat up again the alligator had disappeared—but there, sitting on the stump-end of the fallen tree, was another presence. It seemed to be a man; at least its face was slightly less green and slightly less 'warty than the alligator's had been.

Luther stared up at the stranger.

"Evenin'," he murmured.

"Good evening, son," the stranger replied. "What seems to be the difficulty?"

"Ah fell."

"Hmm, so I perceive. Well, you're not the only one. I've had some previous acquaintance with the fallen." The stranger smiled benignly. "It behooves us, if you'll pardon the expression, to take consolation at times likes these in that glorious motto, 'The South shall rise again!' And now, if you'll permit me to assist you—"

He extended a hand and hauled young Luther up to a seat beside him on the log. Luther blinked at him and beheld his benefactor. The stranger was a plump, white-haired gentleman wearing a hammer-tail coat and a modest five-gallon hat.

"Who mought you be?" Luther inquired.

"I might be Judge Harmer," the stranger told him.

"Judge?"

"An honorary title, of course," his companion assured him. "But I'm a real Harmer, of that you may be sure. Come from a long line of Harmers. Certainly you are familiar with the name?"

"Reckon not," Luther answered. "Ah'm a stranger in these parts. Luther Snodgrass, at yo' service."

"Pleased to meet you." Judge Harmer's eyes twinkled. "But speaking of service, I perceive you have a bottle—"

"He'p yo'self," Luther urged, extending the *Finkola*.

Judge Harmer reached for the bottle, read the label, then hastily drew his hand away. "No, thank you," he muttered. "On second thought—"

"But it's only *Finkola*—"

"I assure you I'm perfectly familiar with the concoction," Judge Harmer replied. "And so again I say, no, thanks."

"You talk awful funny."

"Just plain English."

"Yeah, what I mean. Y'all sound like—pardon the expression—a Yankee." Luther gazed suspiciously at his new acquaintance. "If'n you ain't a real judge, then what are you, anyhow?"

"Call me a talent scout, if you like."

"A talent scout? You mean like for shows and all?"

Judge Harmer nodded.

"Come now!" Luther stood up. "What-all would a talent scout be doin' out heah in this little ole swamp?"

"Why, looking for talent, of course."

"In a bayou—at midnight?"

"I was informed that there might be a possibility of an informal get-together in these purlieus," the judge explained.

"Who-all would hold a sociable in a place like this?" Luther's eyes narrowed. "Hold on—you-all ain't talkin' about one of them Voodoo meetin's, are you?"

THE JUDGE shrugged. "I believe I've heard the term used in that connection, yes."

"But what kind of talent can you git out'n a bunch of conjure men and hexers?"

"Oh, you'd be surprised." The judge smiled. "I understand they sing and dance at such ceremonies. And of course, there are always drummers. There's a great demand for drummers up North, you know. Give a man a set of bongoes instead of a drum and clap a beret on his head and you've got a good non-union Beatnik."

"Nevah figgered it that way befo'," Luther admitted.

"But I fear I was mistaken," the judge continued, consulting his pocket-watch. Luther couldn't imagine how he could possibly see it in the darkness, but apparently the green and glittering eyes searched out successfully. "Here it is, past midnight, and no meeting in evidence." He sighed. "I don't know what's come over folks nowadays, really I don't! Used to be an average of three meetings a week, regular as clockwork, and a human sacrifice on Sundays. Now everybody stays home and watches Oral Roberts on television." He sighed again. "Apparently I'm wasting my time."

"Hold on!" Luther said. "If it's talent you're after, mebbe Ah'm your boy. If'n Ah kin find mah *git*-tar—"

He stooped and fumbled in the mud at his feet until he located the battered instrument. Raising it, he brushed his fingers lightly across the strings, then turned the guitar and shook it vigorously.

"Dern that toad!" he muttered, then brightened. "Happens that Ah'm a entetainer mah-self. You-all care for an audition?"

"Be delighted." The judge settled himself on the log and Luther, without further preamble, launched into the rendition of a popular ditty entitled *The Hang Down Your Head Tom Dooley Cha-Cha-Cha.*

Several alligators back in the swamp joined in the second chorus, and Luther finished with a brisk *obligato* that caromed off his left tonsil.

"Well?" he inquired. "What do you think?"

"I think I'll have a drink after all," said the judge, hastily reaching for the *Finkola* bottle.

"You didn't like mah singin'?"

"I never said that," his audience replied. "In fact, I was merely about to propose a toast."

"What about mah playin'?"

"I never heard anything to equal it." The judge took a deep gulp.

"Mebbe you-all'd like to give me a job?"

"My dear boy, I'm no impresario!"

"Is that like an imp, mebbe?"

"In a way." The judge smiled. "Actually, an impresario is a bit worse—he's a man who puts on theatrical performances. Well, as I say, I'm not one of those. I'm merely a sort of talent scout. I only find talent."

"An agent, like?"

"Ah, yes. That would be closer to the truth. I'm an agent."

"Then you could sign me up?"

"Well—"

"Mebbe you ain't convinced. Mebbe Ah ought to sing agin—"

"No!" the judge exclaimed, hurriedly. "No, that won't be necessary at all. I'm quite willing to sign you right now."

"Ten per cent, ain't it?"

"A hundred per cent, if you like."

"That's moughty generous," Luther grinned. "One o' them long-term contracks?"

"Lifetime," the judge assured him. "Better still, in perpetuity."

"Ah was kinda hopin' we could sign right heah."

"Good enough." The judge produced a document—not from his pocket, not from his sleeve, but from somewhere around his person. "Errr—I seem to have mislaid my fountain-pen. But this twig will do. And for ink, let's just prick your finger, here."

"Nothin' doin'!" Luther drew himself proudly erect. "Ah suspicioned you-all was the Devil right along."

"But I'm not the Devil, I swear it—merely an agent!" The judge's tones were unctuous. "Son, this is your big chance. Don't toss it away because of a technicality!"

"Well, Ah ain't signin' anythin' in mah blood." Luther frowned determinedly, then brightened. "Lookee heah, how's about me signin' in some of this *Finkola?*"

"Hmmm—I don't know—it seems to me to be highly irregular—"

"Ain't nothin' irregular about it!" Luther protested. "Ah done heah the raddio announcer tell just the opposite. He say there ain't nothin' like *Finkola* for keepin' you *regular.*"

"I'd prefer blood," the judge murmured.

"You-all want me or don't you?" Luther was solemn. "Ah tell you, friend, it ain't every day you git a chance to heah a talent like mine. You better not pass it by."

The judge sighed. "That's right," he said.

"So what you say?"

The judge sighed again. "Oh, very well. Sign in *Finkola*. After what you've already drunk from the bottle, I'm sure your blood is probably ninety per cent *Finkola* anyway. So there's not much difference."

"You-all want this formal?" Luther inquired. "If so, Ah'll make a capital X."

"Can't you write?" The judge frowned. "Not even your own name?"

"Course Ah kin! It's the spellin' Ah ain't so sure of." Luther scrawled his X on the document, then reached for the bottle.

"We got us a deal," he said. "Mought as well kill this now."

Apparently the *Finkola* had the same idea, because shortly after swallowing it, Luther gazed at his newfound agent with a contented grin, rolled up his eyes and heels, and passed out.

CHAPTER THREE

When he came to, he was in Noiseville, U.S.A.

Now the actual name of the town may be Nashville, or Chattanooga, or even Memphis. All three communities have at times proclaimed—and loudly— their right to be called the music capitals of America.

Call it rock-in-roll, call it country music, call it hillbilly style, call it something which can't be printed in these pages—the fact remains that these three cities are responsible for more popular entertainment, decibel for decibel, and dollar for dollar, than any other metropolises since Sodom and Gomorrah.

And it was in one of them that Luther Snodgrass awoke.

"Where am Ah?" he wailed.

"Does it matter?" replied Judge Harmer.

"Matter? Ah'll say it does! Must've been drunk as a skunk! Ah do declare, Ah don't even remember mah own name."

"It's Clay Clinton," the judge told him.

"Clay Clinton?" The young man blinked suspiciously. "You sure it ain't Luther Snodgrass?"

"Not after last night it isn't. Don't you remember? You auditioned for me, I signed you up as my client?"

"Yeah, reckon so."

"Well, as your agent, I'm taking over your career. And the first thing I'm doing is changing your name.

Luther Snodgrass—that's no good for theater marquees. Takes too many lights. And it's too long for TV credit cards. You're Clay Clinton."

"Ah'm goin' on television?"

"Eventually. After you've had your vocal lessons."

"Ah don't need none. Ah sing okay."

"I'm not referring to singing. You're going to learn English."

"But who kin unnerstan' Elvis or Jerry Lee Lewis—?"

"I'm not referring to the way you deliver the so-called lyrics of your so-called songs.

It's just that when you talk, it helps to be intelligible."

"You gonna ruin mah style."

"Trust me. From now on you're Clay Clinton, and you're my boy."

"He's *my* boy!"

For the first time Luther heard the strange voice.

He raised his head (he was lying in bed in Room 666 of the Flabbee Arms Hotel at the time) and instantly regretted his effort. It made his skull ache with a hangover, and worse than that, it afforded him a glimpse of the speaker.

A dear little white-haired old lady stood at the judge's side, smiling lovingly at Luther from behind the neck of a gin bottle. She gazed at him with tender, bloodshot eyes.

"Son," said the judge. "I want you to meet your mother."

"Mother'?" Luther sat up. "Not really?"

"Don't ever let me catch you talking like that again," the judge cautioned him. "From now on, you're Clay Clinton, like I said. And this is your dear mother."

"But—"

"It's time, son, that you learned the Facts of Life. Every young popular singing star has a mother, whom he worships and adores. Not only is it good for reams of publicity, but it can also help to take the heat off if—perish forbid!—he happens to get tangled up with one of those chorus girls in Las Vegas. You understand?"

Luther nodded. "So you hired me a mother, is that it?"

He stared at the little old lady. "Where'd she park her broomstick?"

"If you must know, it's on the roof," the little old lady told him. "My cat is watching it. She's queer for phallic symbols."

"Then you *are* a witch?" Luther swung his legs over the side of the bed. "Ah was only kiddin.' Ah nevah dreamed—"

"Here, where are you going?" the judge demanded.

"Away!" Luther fumbled for his jeans. "Ah don't aim to mess with no witches—"

"We have a contract," Judge Harmer reminded him. "Besides, she's not a practicing witch. She's retired."

"That's right, buster," cackled the old woman. "The judge hired me right out of the Old Spook's Home."

"But Ah don't need no super-type-natural Mamma."

"No. But you do need an English instructor. And that's something your new mother can do for you. She can teach you how to speak properly. Besides, I want someone around here to keep all eye on you while I'm away."

"You goin' somewheres?"

"Of course. I'm an agent. You're not my only client, you know. I've got people in New York, Miami, Hollywood, who need my help. But ask your mother. She can tell you."

And in the days that followed, she did.

CHAPTER FOUR

Mother proved to be an apt instructor. During the next few weeks, the new Clay Clinton stayed in his room with her and she patiently taught him the rudiments of grammar and pronunciation. Using such standard texts as *Downbeat* and *Variety,* he gradually enlarged his vocabulary.

The judge appeared three weeks later.

"Well?" he inquired. "How is it going?"

"Crazy, man!" Luther informed him. "Mom falls up to the pad here, making the scene with the English bit every day, and I'm coming on strong. I mean, it's like a gasser, Dad. You dig?"

The judge beamed. "My boy, I'm proud of you!" he declared. "All that vulgar Southern accent has disappeared—now anyone can understand what you're saying. Son, I do believe you're almost ready."

"Almost? Like I'm the most, Daddy-O." Luther paced the floor. "I'm with it, Pops. Solid."

"Not so fast. First we'll have to work on your musical education."

"What's with the music, Clyde? I make with my pipes, I belt it out and they flip. I mean like they'll love it."

The judge shook his head. "You need polish. That's another thing Mother is here to teach you." He turned to the little old lady. "Let him study for another couple of weeks," he commanded. "With the cat."

"The cat? Which cat?"

"My black cat," Mother told him. "She's got just the right *vibrato* for a popular singer these days. Real fish-shaped tones."

So for two weeks, Luther listened to the cat. The cat didn't always feel like howling, but mother belted it regularly with her broomstick and belted herself with the gin bottle as Luther listened and learned.

When the judge returned he was properly impressed. Luther did a number for him.

"Wonderful," Judge Harmer exclaimed. "Why, you can't hardly tell him and the cat apart!"

"He's a good boy," mother declared. "You know, Judge, I had my doubts when you took me out of straight sorcery and made me get into show biz. I thought you were like putting me down. But this is the greatest! Sticking pins into wax figures, all that jazz—it's funky compared to working with live talent. And when I think of all the harm I can do—"

She cackled and tackled her gin.

"Never mind that now," the judge cautioned, with a warning look in Luther's direction. "We're going to put the finishing touches on his education now. I think we're ready for Eddie."

"Eddie?" Luther echoed. "Who's he?"

"Eddie Puss, at your service—blowing cool and plenty nervous!" A dapper little bald-headed man bounded into the room. "Ah, Mother, good to see you! Share some skin!" He shook hands enthusiastically.

"Same old fascinating witch, eh? Have broom, will travel. Righterooni?"

"This is Eddie Puss," the judge said. "He writes songs."

"Not my real name, of course," the little man said, grinning at Luther. "They slapped the handle on me because I write a lot of *Mother* numbers. Eddie Puss, like in the complex and all that jazz, dig? Also, because I'm quite a cat."

"But I don't need a songwriter," Luther objected, in his newfound English. "I'm the most."

"Everybody needs songwriters in this business," the judge told him. "How do you suppose a hit singer operates these days? They all have to write their own numbers in order to get into the Top Ten. And that's where people like Eddie come in handy. They can do the coaching. Teach you the ropes." He turned to the little man. "How about it—what do you think?"

"Well, I don't know." Eddie Puss surveyed Luther with a calculating eye. "He's almost too old, don't you think? I mean, what we need like is young blood. Most big hits, they're written by kids still in high school. Freshmen are best. Me, I've even worked with seniors, but it's hard."

"He's really very childish," the judge reassured him. "I want you to try."

"I can't promise anything—"

"You wouldn't be going back on our agreement, would you?" The judge was suave. "Remember what you were when I met you? Just a frustrated lyric-writer. All you ever were able to do was those four-line poems on the walls of public—"

"Never mind!" Eddie Puss shuddered. "I appreciate what you've done, and like I say, I'll try."

"Then get busy," the judge muttered. "I want this boy in shape for his debut in two weeks. Teach him the popular song business."

So Luther learned the popular song business from yet another teacher.

"Really nothing to it," Eddie reassured him, during the course of their daily lessons. "It's as simple as NBC. All you got to remember is that there are only two kinds of pop hits today. One of 'em is about a couple of high school kids in love, and the other makes even less sense. The main thing is, you have to remember to include certain phrases in each lyric."

"Such as?"

"Well, We got what we call keywords. You know 'em."

"You mean like *heart,* and *tears,* and *embrace?*"

"Crazy, man! Only you never use 'em that way. You make with the phrase. So it comes out, *this heart of mine,* and *these tears in my eyes,* and *your fond embrace.* Whatever you do, never change a single word. Here's the rest of the list—dig it, because it's all you're gonna need to write dozens of songs. *The touch of your lips. They don't understand. I hold your charms. Each thrilling moment. Of love divine.*" He paused. "And one thing more. The most important bit. Every couple of lines, you got to throw in the word, *baby.*"

Mother was crying. "I always was one to snap my cap over poetry."

Luther himself was equally impressed.

"See how easy it is?" Eddie remarked. "With me helping you on lyrics and the cat here giving you the tunes, we can't miss."

And they didn't.

TWO WEEKS later, to the day, Judge Harmer appeared in the hotel room.

"Everything in readiness?" he demanded. Mother and Eddie Puss beamed proudly and the cat purred at Luther and nodded.

"Prepare to dig your wig, Big Daddy," Luther said, picking up his guitar. "We've got a smasheroo."

And he launched into the world premiere of the number now universally known as, *If I Had To Do It All Over Again, I'd Do It All Over You.*

For a moment after the last note sickened and died away there was an impressive silence in the little room.

Then the telephone jingled and Judge Harmer picked it up.

"Yes," he said. "Yes, I understand. Right away."

He replaced the phone in its cradle and turned to the gathering with a smile of relief.

"Management is getting complaints on the noise," he said, happily. "We're being evicted."

"Then it registered," Eddie Puss muttered.

"It must have. Come on, let's get started."

"Where are we going?" Luther was puzzled.

"To New York, of course. For your debut. I understand that Hank Corrupta is replacing Terry Coma at the Club Sandwich on Saturday."

"Corrupta? He's with that rival outfit, MCA, isn't he?" Eddie demanded.

"Right. We got to get rid of him. And we will."
Judge Harmer grinned. "What he doesn't know is that
our boy here will be replacing him."

"But how——?" Luther murmured.

"You'll see." The judge turned. "Start packing, we're
off to the big city."

Mother started for the window.

"Where are you going?" the judge demanded.

"I was just after my broomstick——"

"We're traveling by TWA this time," he told her.
"Never mind the expense. Besides, I'll need your
services *en route.*"

"What do you want me to do?"

"Get three pounds of wax—no, two will do.
Corrupta's pretty skinny. Make me a puppet. And
then——"

"With the pins, eh? Give him the old stab-and-jab
routine?" Mother cackled.

"No, he wouldn't even feel the needle. He'd just
think it was a fast fix. I've got a better idea." And the
judge whispered something in her ear.

She cackled again.

And she continued to cackle on the plane, as she sat
beside Luther and molded a wax figurine, which took on
an eerie resemblance to Hank Corrupta.

"Why, it's amazing!" Luther marveled. "Where did
you ever learn to model like that?"

"In my younger days I used to work for Disney," the
crone confided. "I was a stand-in for *The Reluctant
Dragon.* I picked up a lot of techniques from his artists."

"Well, it's certainly a remarkable job," the young man
said. "Even those hands are perfect."

"They have to be," the old woman said. "Because of this." She began to mumble over the mannequin and then, suddenly, she reached out and squeezed the waxen right hand.

"You—you *crushed* it!"

Luther exclaimed.

"Natch. And I just got you a job!" she predicted.

Luther didn't believe it.

CHAPTER FIVE

Not until he arrived in New York and Judge Harmer showed him the announcement in Ed Sullivan's column. Hank Corrupta would not be opening at the Club Sandwich on Saturday night after all.

"Lost his voice?" Luther wondered, aloud.

"Worse than that," the judge declared, smugly. "Read what it says. He can't sing because he hurt his hand and he won't be able to snap his fingers!"

"But I still don't see—"

"Leave everything to me. I'm going down to the Club Sandwich right now and talk to the boys about putting you on."

"You have connections?"

"In this business, you've got to have connections. Why, the Musician's Union and I are just like that." He held up two fingers, then drew them across his throat.

Luther shivered.

He was still shivering after the judge had left.

"What's the matter, boy?" asked Eddie Puss. "What gives?"

"I'm scared," Luther confessed.

"What's to be scared of? You're all set. You've let your sideburns grow, you haven't combed your hair in a month, and if you shiver like that on stage tonight nobody can tell you from Elvis himself."

"It's not that. It's like I never really believed what the judge said before. And I never thought mother was a real witch—"

"Wise up, buster," the old woman said. "How do you think anyone gets ahead in show business these days? It sure enough ain't talent."

"You mean it's all the result of magic?"

"What do you think? You've watched television, haven't you? How else could half of those ham-bones get on in the first place?"

"But I've always thought—"

"Never mind what you thought. This is it, pal. This is the big time!"

And it was.

THAT EVENING evening, at ten o'clock, Luther Snodgrass, *alias* Clay Clinton, stepped up to the microphone of the Club Sandwich and brandished the gold guitar that Judge Harmer had slipped into his surprised fingers just before his number was announced.

And he killed the people.

"I did it!" Luther marveled, at the impromptu party following his performance. "I really sent them!" He laughed happily and nudged Eddie Puss in the ribs. "And it was me, singing and playing up there. That's what they dug the most—me. Nobody hoodooed them into applauding. And to think I almost fell for that line about witchcraft!"

"Yeah," said Eddie.

"You were ribbing me, weren't you? I mean, you're just a lyric writer. The judge is a smart agent, but he's only human. Mother gets stoned and thinks she's a witch, but that's for the birds. I see it now—you were all in it together, a real swinging combo, feeding me that jazz so I'd keep up my confidence."

"Yeah," said mother.

"But from now on, we're straight up and flying right. I get the message—you can level with me. Because I'm not scared any more. I know I can punch over a number. So let's forget all that Creepville jazz."

"Yeah," said the cat...

AND LUTHER Snodgrass forgot witchcraft from then on. In a little while he almost forgot his own name. Because he was Clay Clinton now, and there wasn't time to think about anything else.

Judge Harmer kept him busy.

First of all, there was the recording bit.

"Records," the judge told him. "That's where the big loot is made. I'm going to get you into every juke-box in the country."

"But I'm not even signed with a recording outfit," Luther protested.

"Who needs it?" Eddie Puss demanded. "What we do is, we set up our own waxworks. That way we don't just collect the royalties—we get profit on distribution, the whole package."

"But how can we be sure the records will become popular? How can we get them spinning?"

"Through the deejays," Eddie told him. "They can make you or break you."

"Can Judge Harmer get the disc-jockeys to play our waffles?"

Eddie Puss smiled grimly. "Believe me," he said, "some of his best friends are disc jockeys. When it comes to going after a fast buck, he doesn't care who he associates with or how low he stoops!"

And so Clay Clinton's gold guitar was matched by his growing collection of gold records. Remember his clever modern adaptation of great classical favorites— *Rock-'n-Roll Of Ages* and *When The Rock-'n-Roll Is Called Up Yonder* and all the rest? Or would you rather forget?

The point is, the public didn't forget. It never had a chance to do so. Clay Clinton was on every radio show. Clay Clinton was in every jukebox. Clay Clinton moved from the Club Sandwich to top spots in Chicago, Detroit, St. Louis, Miami. Clay Clinton appeared in theaters and auditoriums. Clay Clinton guested for his fan clubs. Clay Clinton did his act on the U.S.A. *Grandstand* television show, and two fourteen-year-old girls tore off his pink shoelaces for souvenirs.

He acquired a wardrobe of sixty suits and a fleet of nine Cadillac convertibles, and eventually reached such heights of success that he was seriously thinking about going to a psychiatrist.

But he just didn't have the time. There was never any time, any more.

Eddie Puss had long since dropped out of sight. "You don't need him," the judge decided. "From now on, you plug standard tunes. Besides, I've got other assignments for him to handle."

That was something Luther had learned; he was indeed far from the only client Judge Harmer dealt with. It seemed, in his travels through the enchanted realms of show business, that the judge had connections everywhere. Although he specialized in teenage talent, it almost appeared as though teenagers had taken over the bulk of the entertainment outlets in the country. Between rock-'n-roll singers and progressive jazz combos, they dominated the musical end, and there was little else.

"Of course, there's the movies to be considered," the judge said, thoughtfully. "I've got something working for me out there."

"You mean you're active in Hollywood too?" Luther marveled.

"Why not? Who do you think is responsible for all those pictures about juvenile delinquents? If it wasn't for the how-to-do-it movies, the average kid wouldn't know how to handle a switch-blade or smoke a reefer."

"You're kidding, of course," Luther said.

"And then there's the monster movies," the judge went on. "That's a pretty important department. You know the kind—*I Was A Teen-Age Supreme Court Justice,* and *Invasion of the Giant Spirochetes?* I've been promoting them pretty heavily, and with fine results. Ten years ago there was a lot of silly talk about motion picture audiences with a mental age of twelve. Well, we've made a lot of progress since then. I think we've got it down to around seven. Of course, this doesn't include western fans or Mickey Spillane addicts, or the people who think a girl is hiding her talent if she wears a brassiere. If we included them, we'd have the index of intelligence down to about five years of age."

"I doubt it," Luther mused.

"Well, I can dream, can't I?" the judge retorted.

"Look here," said Luther. "You aren't serious, are you? You don't really want to put out all this crud? I mean, in my spare time between shows, I've been doing quite a bit of reading on my own—"

"Reading?" The judge raised his eyebrows. "Mother had strict orders to keep you on *Billboard* and *Mad Comics.*"

"Mother isn't around much," Luther confessed. "When all this loot started pouring in she came to me and hinted about retiring. Said it wasn't so much her idea as it was the cat's. It seems like the cat had always wanted to settle down in a little vine-covered cottage and raise mice for a hobby. And for twenty thousand dollars, mother found just the place—not exactly a cottage, but a lovely old liquor store. She said that with all that wine and stuff around she wouldn't need any vines. So I bought it for her, and she cut out."

"Leaving you to read, eh?" The judge frowned.

"Well, like why not? I mean, I dig education the most. I figure education is one of the best forms of learning, particularly if you want to know something. And like that there."

"It's corrupting your taste, son. Pretty soon it will affect your art."

"I meant to flip my lip about that, too." Luther sighed.

"You know, sometimes I wonder if all this singing I do is really the living end. I get to thinking it's cornball. Now you take this character Boris Pasternak and what he says about the artistic conscience bit—"

"Look." Judge Harmer put his hand on Luther's shoulder. "You're a singer. I'm your agent. I made you.

I have further plans. Your only job is to carry them out."

"But why? I'm making plenty of money now. I could retire on royalties. And you've got other clients, a lot of them."

"It isn't a question of money. It's a question of ethics."

"Ethics?"

"Sure, what else have we been talking about? Ethics—I want to degrade them. I won't rest until the whole world is rocking and rolling."

"But why?"

"Because it's my duty, that's why. Just as it's mother's duty to be a respectable, practicing witch instead of running off to lush it up in a liquor store. Not that I have anything against lushes, understand—they're quite acceptable, in a way. But the major task comes first. To corrupt, and to destroy."

Luther grinned. "So you're back to that old line again," he said. "Trying to scare me with that phony superstition talk. Well, it won't work. I've come a long way since you met me in the swamp."

"And you can go right back there if you aren't careful," the judge retorted. "Very well, I have no intention of convincing you that I'm an emissary of infernal powers. Just let me say this, though—when you argue against bad taste, you're arguing against your own bread and butter, to say nothing of the necessities of life, such as caviar and champagne. Forget all this nonsense about self-improvement."

"But I don't want to forget—"

"Then remember this. You and I have a contract. And according to the terms, I'm entitled to plan your itinerary. From now on I'll see to it that you're so busy you won't have time to read or moon around with a lot of egghead ideas, either."

The judge stood up. "Start packing," he said. "I'm taking you right to the Home Office." He frowned grimly.

Luther gulped. "Now, look here," he said. "Don't put me down."

"Put you down? That's a good one." Judge Harmer chuckled gutturally.

"It isn't that I believe you, or anything," Luther quavered. "But you keep talking about the Home Office. I understand that the climate in Hell is pretty bad."

The judge laughed again. "Who said anything about Hell? Where I'm taking you, the climate is even worse. This is the twentieth century, son, and we move with the times. Our Home Office is in Hollywood!"

CHAPTER SIX

Luther Snodgrass was in Hollywood for exactly three days when he met Mary Jane Hawkins. He happened to be sitting in the outer office of Judge Harmer's agency office on Vermont when the girl walked in.

He watched the little blonde request an interview from the receptionist, and saw her receive the usual brush-off—the *don't-call-us-we'll-call-you* routine. He noted how her shoulders sagged, and noted too how other salient portions of her anatomy remained fascinatingly firm.

Then she turned away, and saw him sitting there, and something happened.

It was hate at first sight. "Clay Clinton!" the girl exclaimed. "Aaargh!"

"What?" said Luther, rising to his feet.

"Aaargh!" the little blonde repeated. "Also pfaugh!"

"I don't dig you, chick."

Mary Jane moved closer and peered up at him. "You *are* Clay Clinton, aren't you?"

"Well—like yes, I guess so."

"Then blecchhh," she told him. "To say nothing of bracchhh. And, if you'll pardon the expression, *pfui!*"

"Now wait a minute, doll. Listen to me—"

"I *have* listened to you," Mary Jane told him. "Which is precisely what I mean when I say—"

"Let's not go through that routine again," Luther said, hastily. "It hurts me to hear such sounds coming out of a lush thrush like you."

"You're a fine one to talk," the girl retorted. "What about the sounds *you* make?"

"Are you knocking my singing?" Luther demanded.

"Singing!" She sighed dismally. "That's what you call it, eh?"

"Well, I may not be the greatest," Luther admitted, "but it's a living. I mean, I got nine Cadillacs, and—"

"Sure. You've got nine Cadillacs. And meanwhile, a girl like me can't even get an audition from an agent. That's because I have a trained voice and all the public wants to hear nowadays is a lot of screeching. You and your kind are responsible for that."

"Now don't make a federal case out of it," Luther murmured. "Don't hang me, judge!"

"I wish I could. I happen to love music, and when I think of what you've done to ruin singing in this country, I could just scream."

"In what key?"

"Now you're making fun of me." Mary Jane stamped her foot petulantly, and it was Luther who screamed, because she came down on his toes.

"Ohh—I'm sorry—I didn't mean to lose my temper—"

"That's all right," Luther told her.

"I apologize for being so rude."

"You only told the truth."

"What?" She stared at him.

"I know I can't sing," Luther said.

"But—"

"Let me explain." He smiled at her. "Kind of a long story, so I won't do a standup routine. How about lunch?"

CADILLAC NUMBER Seven (the pink one, with the purple upholstery) happened to be on the parking lot outside, and he drove her to the Derby. And it was there that he told her the story.

"I can't believe it," she murmured, shaking her head slowly.

"This is Truthville, U.S.A.," Luther insisted.

"But it's fantastic!" Mary Jane wrinkled her forehead. "It's absurd to think of the Devil trying to take over the entertainment and television industry in this town! Besides, he wouldn't have a chance, as long as Desi Arnaz is around."

"I didn't go for the bundle myself, really," Luther confessed. "Not until Judge Harmer brought me out here and I dug what went on around his office. In the past couple of days I've seen him do business with half the weirdies in show biz."

He described some of the no-talent he'd met—the orchestra leaders who couldn't read music and their musicians who couldn't play a note as written—the offbeat young actors from the torn-shirt schools of drama who seemed to have a madness in their method—the dancers whose movements depended less on choreography than on the tightness of their underwear.

"All right," Mary Jane conceded. "I know a lot of these people are bad. But that doesn't mean they're part of some organized conspiracy. Aren't you exaggerating just a trifle?"

Luther shook his head earnestly. "Has to be a plot," he insisted. "How else would all those idiot M.C.s get jobs on those daytime giveaway shows? Where do all the loudmouthed announcers come from with their pitches for pile remedies?"

"But surely it's not the Devil's work?"

"Oh, no?" Luther stared at her triumphantly. "Who do you think invented the singing commercial?"

"Well—"

The girl was weakening.

"You heard how I got into this racket," Luther continued. "Judge Harmer admitted he was an agent, didn't he? He laid it on me about how he was out to ruin the public's taste. It figures."

"Yes, it figures." Mary Jane nodded at him. "You're a nice person, Clay. I misjudged you."

"Call me Luther," he begged.

"All right—Luther. I'm ashamed of the way I acted when we met. Now that you've told me your story, I think I'm beginning to understand the situation. And I'd like to help you."

"You can't help me," Luther said. "I never knew until recently that I was no good, and that the reason I was hired was just because I was so terrible. But it's too late to do anything about that now. I'm under contract."

"Contracts can be broken."

"This one is in perpetuity." Luther smiled and shrugged. "When the judge told me that, I thought he was talking about a place. Since then I've done a little reading, you know? I'm up on all this longhair talk."

"Like paranoid delusions, for example?"

"Huh?"

"Like sick-sick-sick," the girl explained, patiently. "Rationalizing your sudden success into a diabolical conspiracy."

"Stop making like a square," Luther begged her. "All I know is, I've got a contract. I'm hooked."

"You really believe this?"

"If I don't, may I drop dead and work for Lawrence Welk."

Mary Jane bit her lip. "Please—watch your language."

"I'm sorry."

"I'm sorry, too." She gazed at him for a long moment. "Well, if there is something to what you say, then maybe there's a way out."

"Like what?"

"Perhaps you need to be exorcised."

"I get all the exercise I need at the hotel swimming pool."

"Not exercise—*exorcise*. That means to cast out demons."

"You mean there's a way to get rid of the Devil?"

"I wouldn't know. But I do know there are a lot of psychic mediums in this town. Some of them claim to be able to communicate with spirits. Suppose you went to one and presented your problem? Maybe something could be done."

"But I wouldn't know where to find a cat like that."

"Let's try the Yellow Pages."

And sure enough, in one of the five phonebooks of Greater Los Angeles, they discovered Dunn.

CHAPTER SEVEN

Medium Dunn turned out to be a little old man who operated a spiritualist parlor on Fairfax, above one of those used-clothing shops that specialized in selling the discarded costumes of motion picture stars. There was a big sale on leopard-skin trusses left over from an old Tarzan movie in the downstairs section, but up above all was quiet.

Little Mr. Dunn listened to Luther's story in silence and seemed not at all surprised at his client's revelations.

"Do you think you can help him?" Mary Jane asked.

"I'm not sure." The little old man cupped his hand to his ear. "Who did you say it was held your contract?"

"Judge Harmer. At least, that's what he calls himself."

"Judge Harmer." The cupped hand trembled perceptibly. "I was afraid I'd heard the name."

"Then you know him?"

"Yes. He's got quite a reputation in certain circles."

"Could you exorcise his influence?"

Medium Dunn shook his head slowly. "Judge Harmer is mighty big in this town," he said. "Mighty big. He's got quite a large and dependent following."

"Then there's nothing you can do?"

"I didn't say that." Medium Dunn peered out of the window at the pink Cadillac. "For a reasonable offering—say a thousand dollars—I can put you in touch with certain parties who have the power to negotiate. Mind you, I couldn't help you break the contract; I can't promise that. All I can do is open the way for a meeting."

"A conference?"

"You might call it that."

"When? Where?"

"Now. And right here. If you happen to have the thousand on you. Or are you one of those people who never carry more than fifty dollars in cash?"

"I never signed for those ads," Luther told him, pulling out an alligator billfold and prying open its jaws. "Here's the loot."

Medium Dunn glanced at the girl. "I'm going to ask you to step outside and wait," he said.

Mary Jane departed for the reception room and settled down with a bundle of old psychic magazines. She buried her nose in a copy of The Saturday Evening Ghost and kept it there, even when the smell of burning sulfur issued from behind the closed doors. She could hear the scraping of chalk on the floor and the sound of an eerie chant. Then there was silence.

Inside the darkened room, Luther Snodgrass lay on a couch. He too could smell the sulfur, hear the chalk tracing a curious geometrical figure that resembled nothing so much as a pentagram with two pairs of pents. And then he listened to the chanting. His eyes closed, and the chanting rose to a faint and far-off wail. The smoke rose around him in the darkness. And then—

And then he was rising, not to walk but to swoop through space. He was rising, or was he falling? He didn't know, because all at once there were no directions any more; no up, no down. But Luther moved, moved through blackness into deeper night. And there was a circle of light that moved with him, supporting his substance until he stood silently before the shadows.

Behind the shadows were stars, and he realized then that he must be in outer space.

"I'm way out," he said.

THE SHADOWS stirred. Stirred and blurred. Blurred and brightened.

Now he could see the enormous outlines of the crouching figures, stare into the gigantic eyes that held all emptiness. There were two figures, four eyes. He faced them, puzzlement overriding panic.

"Two?" he muttered to himself. "I always thought there was only one—"

"There is one," came the reply. *"But he is not here. We are but judges."*

"Judges? What do I need with a judge?"

"You wish to discuss a contract, is that not so?"

"Yes."

"Then it is a matter of law, and judges are required."

"I never thought of it that way."

"We will hear your plea."

"Well—"

"Proceed. There is no time to waste. The Devil will find work for idle hands to do." Two pairs of gigantic hands reached towards Luther's neck, and he retreated hastily to the center of the circle of light.

"I get the message," he said, shuddering. "But it's really just a simple bit. You see, there's this deal I have on with Judge Harmer, if you happen to know him—"

"We know him. He is our brother."

"Ullp! Your brother, eh?"

Luther hesitated, then plunged on. "Well, we had this little agreement, dig? Only now I want out. That's all there is to it. I want out."

"You signed a contract?"

"Uh—yes."

"Then you are committed. There is no legal way to free yourself of obligation unless he releases you."

"But couldn't you persuade him?"

"Why should we?"

"Can't I buy my way out?"

"With what?"

"Money. Loot. Moola. Look. I'm loaded. I've got nine Cadillacs—"

"What do we want with your Cadillacs? We do not run a used car lot. Although, naturally, we do business with many used car dealers."

There was faint amusement in the booming voice, but none in Luther's quivering whisper.

"But there must be some way I can lick this thing. If you don't want money, what do you want?"

There was a long pause until the voices came again.

"We do not buy."

"We do not sell."

"But at times we trade."

"Trade what?"

"An eye for an eye. A tooth for a tooth."

"I didn't sell any eyes or teeth."

"We know what you sold."

"So shall we say—a soul for a soul?"

"Another soul in exchange for mine? But whose—"

"There is a girl. One who trusts you."

"Now, hold it—"

"If you were to take her to Judge Harmer, she would go willingly enough. You could tell her you were mistaken about him, that it was all a delusion on your part. You would say that you were using your influence to secure her an opportunity. It could be arranged for the judge to offer her a contract. Once she signs, you are released."

"That would be a fair exchange."

"Like hell it would! Nothing doing!"

"Then your plea is dismissed."

"But—"

"Go."

The huge hands reached forth. And the voices boomed.

"A final warning. Do not attempt to evade your contract. This time you have come to us. But next time we can come to you."

The hands swooped down and Luther moved. He blurred his way through darkness and then he was falling into the endless emptiness beyond the stars. Falling back on the couch in the little room. Yes, he was there once more, and awake. He could smell the sulfur.

Only it wasn't sulfur, now. It was something else. Something like brimstone

"How'd you make out?" Medium Dunn inquired.

Luther blinked and sat up. "You mean you don't know?" he asked. "You didn't see them, or hear them?"

"I noted nothing," the little old man said. "You appeared to be in a deep trance. Quite similar to that of a hypnotic subject." He brightened. "I happen to be a competent hypnotist, too," he continued. "In case you are ever in need of such services—"

"Never mind," Luther said, rising.

"I am adept at Reichian psychotherapy," Dunn said. "Orgone treatments day or night, by appointment."

"Not interested."

"Tea leaf readings?" Medium Dunn grasped his arm as he hastened towards the door. "How about a high colonic—?"

"Let's get out of here," Luther gasped, pulling Mary Jane to her feet and leading her over to the stairway.

"You might stop downstairs," Medium Dunn called hopefully. "Tell them I sent you and get a ten per cent discount. I understand they have something special in Jayne Mansfield's old bras—"

CHAPTER EIGHT

THE SMOG was reddening into sunset as they reached the street. Luther opened the door of the Caddy and helped the girl to enter.

"How did it go?" she asked. "What happened?"

"Wait," he said. "I don't want to talk here."

They drove in silence up through the hills. In spite of what the TV comics say, it is possible to find a certain serenity in the darkness on Mulholland Drive. And it was there, gazing down across the neon nonentity that is the city, that Luther told Mary Jane of his experience.

"Or was it a dream?" he concluded. "I don't know."

"In any case, you protected me," the girl said. "I'm proud of you."

"I'm not proud," Luther answered, "I'm scared. If it was just a cooky dream, then I'm flipping. And if it happens to be real, well—"

"Forget it," Mary Jane commanded.

"How?"

She showed him. Nice girl or no, Mulholland Drive has a magic all its own. And as she entered his arms, Luther murmured, "Don't worry, baby. I won't let anybody hurt you. And I'm going to get out of this deal, wait and see—"

Suddenly he froze. For there was no need to wait and see. He was seeing, right now.

He was seeing the neon lights blotted out, obscured by the huge talons that descended from the sky, shoving aside the stars as they scrabbled towards him.

"Honey, what's the matter?" Mary Jane whimpered.

The claws came closer. Luther shuddered.

"They're here," he whispered. "They're watching. They know they can't have you—and they won't let me touch you, either."

"You're imagining these things," the girl reassured him. "I don't see anything."

"I do."

"Look." She sat upright, faced him, grasped his hands.

"You're not well. You ought to get out of here, go away from all this. I'll come with you."

"But—"

"Let me take care of you. I want to."

"We'd be poor." Luther glanced up at the sky nervously.

"Who cares?"

"But you don't know what a raunchy character I was when I was poor. Strictly a no-goodnik. Anything for kicks. I was willing to sell my soul—"

"You're not like that any more. We'd get along. I'm sure we would."

"No." Luther was watching something outside the car. He didn't look at her.

"You don't love me, is that it?"

He looked at her then. "Of course I do. Can't you understand? I *want* to go. But they won't let me. They have a contract. They have plans for me. Me and my lousy voice."

"All right." Mary Jane turned away. "I guess I *do* understand, after all. There's no need to hand me a line about how you hate what you're doing, or dream up any more stories about the Devil. I can take a hint. When it comes to a choice between me and nine Cadillacs—"

"It's not that at all," he protested. "There isn't a Cadillac made that can compare with you. Why, I'd trade them all in for just one—"

"I'm not an automobile dealer," she sniffed. "Just take me home, please."

"But—"

"Please," she repeated, kicking him politely in the shins.

Luther drove her home in silence.

And all the way, the shadowy hands followed him across the sky, and somewhere between the stars the eyes blazed down...

JUDGE HARMER was waiting for him beside the swimming pool at the Beverly Hills Hotel.

"Where have you been, son?" he demanded. "What have you been up to?"

"I—" Luther hesitated, gulping.

"Don't tell me, I already know." Harmer raised a pudgy hand and smiled. "Well, it doesn't matter. I'm sure you've learned your lesson. Now we can just let bygones be bygones and get down to business."

"Business?"

The judge nodded. "I didn't bring you out here for a rest cure," he said. "Though speaking for myself, I could certainly use a black sabbatical. It's time to go to work. I've just been talking to the Boss."

"The Boss?"

"Who else? He's out here, too. Just got in from Las Vegas. And he's a little worried about the opposition."

"What opposition?"

"There are certain signs of good taste creeping into the field, and he doesn't like it. You know, things like Playhouse 90, some of those Sunday egghead shows. And movies are improving, too. We've got to hit, and hit hard. That's where you come in. At midnight, Monday, in my office. He wants to meet you then."

"Supposing I refuse?"

Judge Harmer glanced up at the sky.

"Nice clear weather we're having. I'd hate to see a storm come up over the week end."

Luther sighed. "What does he have in mind for me?"

"First of all, we're lining up a regular television show for you. A full thirty-nine week series, every hour staged like a spectacular. You know the bit—lots of guest stars for you to insult and call by their first names, plenty of novelty acts with chimpanzees. You've seen those dance-numbers they stage where three creeps in tights come out and swish around the singer? Well, money is no object—we're going to hire six creeps for your show! Already lined up a sponsor; he's one of the biggest laxative manufacturers in the business. We're going to have singing commercials, too. Remember all these cigarette programs where big burly guys go around puffing on cigarettes as soon as they've finished wrestling an alligator or jumping from a plane without a parachute? The ones where everybody has a tattoo on the back of his hand? Well, the sponsor came up with a great gimmick. Our guys are going to be tattooed on—hey, what's the matter, son?"

Luther groaned.

"Sounds like hard work, eh? Don't worry. You'll have writers. The best. We'll hire five of 'em just to turn out adlibs for you. The same guys who make up all the jokes about how Ed Sullivan looks like an undertaker, or an undertaker's customer. And that's not all."

"More, yet?"

"Certainly! Boss wants you to make a movie. He's doing the script himself. It's called *I Was A Teen-Age Chicken-Plucker For The—*"

"No!" Luther gasped. "No, not that!"

The judge glanced at the sky again and gestured with his cigar. Something brushed Luther's cheek, and a gigantic shadow blurred past him. There was a great splash in the swimming pool and the water suddenly began to steam.

"Hold it," Judge Harmer said, grasping Luther's collar. "I'd hate to see you fall into that pool. Looks to me like it's full of crocodiles, too—you see?"

Luther took one glance, then turned away. "Monday at midnight, you said?" His voice was dull.

"Right! In my office, remember. That gives you the whole weekend to rest up." Harmer nodded briskly and stepped away. "Well, if you'll excuse me, I have an engagement at Forest Lawn."

"At this hour?"

"The young lady prefers it." Judge Harmer chuckled. "Perhaps you'd care to join us? I'm sure we could dig up a date for you."

Luther shook his head and ran down the path towards his guesthouse.

"See you Monday night, then," the judge called. "Meanwhile, take care of your voice. We're counting on you."

Luther took care of his voice. He used it immediately, to call Mary Jane.

"I'm sorry," he said, over the phone. "I know you're making with the mad bit at me, and this is no time to bother you. But I'm really in trouble, and I've got to talk to someone. Unless you can help me—"

"I'll be right over," said Mary Jane Hawkins.

"Good." Luther glanced out of the window. "I was hoping you'd say that. Somehow, I don't care to go out at night myself. Not right now."

"Stay where you are. I understand."

She came over, just as she promised, and Luther told her the story.

CHAPTER NINE

And then, I think, is when Mary Jane came up with her idea. I say I *think*, but I'm not sure.

You see, I hadn't made the scene yet. In fact, I hadn't even met Luther Snodgrass.

I didn't meet him until Monday night.

That's when he walked into Judge Harmer's office and saw me, sitting all alone behind the big desk.

He stared at me as I checked my watch. It was midnight, right on the head.

His eyes bulged. "You're the boss?" he murmured. *"You?"*

I smiled. "Why not?"

"But—"

"What did you expect, a long red tail?" I laughed and brushed the cigarette ashes from my sports jacket.

"You're just a man, aren't you?" He was utterly deflated. "And here, all along, I've been thinking—"

"I know what you've been thinking." I shrugged. "That's what comes of too much reading, my boy. You've been digging the *Faust* bit, haven't you? And *Damn Yankees,* and *Will Success Spoil Rock Hunter?* and all that jazz. You've got the idea that anyone can sell his soul for talent. Let's face it, you're not talented."

Luther nodded at me. "That's right. But the way I had it figured out, from what Judge Harmer told me, the Devil wasn't interested in real talent. He just wanted to corrupt everyone's taste, spoil their standards. From then on, he would find it easier to influence their morals.

It was all a gigantic plot, and it sounded pretty logical to me. I mean, if the Devil were around today, he'd naturally go into the advertising business, and television, and public relations—"

"Please!" I raised my hand. "I grant you it all sounds logical. And if I were the Devil, I just might encourage people to produce shows like Damn Yankees and the rest, simply to be subtle and put the idea into folks' heads that it's possible to cook up a deal. But I'm not the Devil, as you can plainly see."

"Then Judge Harmer is crazy?"

"Like a fox," I told him. "The judge knows what he's doing. He's lined up a great career for you out here. You're going to come on strong. And that's what I want to talk to you about tonight. First off, the television series—"

"You really are serious about this? Even though you know I'm lousy?"

"Let the great American Public be the ones to decide." I stared at him. "I see you brought your guitar. Good. There's a new number I want you to try—the theme song for the show." I reached into my desk and brought forth a sheaf of sheet music. "Here it is. Brand new tune, be up there in the Top Ten three weeks after you introduce it. Great title, too. *Strontium-90 Daddy, Don't You Fall Out On Me!*"

He took the music and held it awkwardly.

"Prop it against the bookends here and let's give it a try," I said. "Just run through it cold. I don't expect a finished performance—all I want is a general idea."

Luther Snodgrass nodded and raised his guitar. Then he smiled at me, cleared his throat, and began.

I got a finished performance.

And I do mean *finished*.

Standing there in my office, Luther Snodgrass sang as he'd never sung before—he sang *good*.

I couldn't believe my ears.

Out of his mouth came the pear-shaped tones of a trained vocalist. He sounded like a concert artist, and he played the guitar like Segovia.

"There." He put down the guitar. "How'd you like that?"

I didn't answer. I couldn't, for a moment. Then I whispered, "Try something else. Let me hear your old number—*If I Had To Do It All Over Again*—"

So he sang *that*. And it sounded, so help me, wonderful. He was even pronouncing the words so you could understand them.

"Try another," I muttered.

He did a third selection. It was even better. I didn't wait for him to finish but made him stop in mid-chorus.

"What's happened?" I demanded. "What's come over you? Why don't you sing the way you always do?"

"Always *did*," he corrected. "I *can't* sing that way anymore. I've been trained."

"By whom?" I snarled, bitterly. Wait until I get my hands on—"

"Mary Jane taught me," Luther said, happily. "Over the weekend. From now on, I'm going to be a real singer."

"But how could you change in just one weekend? And why can't you change back again?"

"Because she didn't teach me alone." Luther was positively grinning now. "She remembered something Dunn had mentioned."

"Medium Dunn?"

"That's the cat. He said he was also a hypnotist. So she took me to him, and he put me under hypnosis while she coached me. Planted subconscious suggestions, you see? Now I couldn't sing the way I used to, even if I wanted to—"

"Which you don't," I grated, savagely. "Because you know blessed well that with this new voice I can't possibly use you any more. That I'll have to release you from your contract."

"I only did it because I thought you were the Devil," Luther explained. "I just wanted to save my soul."

"You and your square soul! As far as I'm concerned, you can take it and—"

"Then you won't be needing me any longer?"

"Who needs you?" I swiveled away from him. "Look, I'm a businessman. I'm in the entertainment field and what I want is mediocrity. Fortunately, there's plenty of it around, just as awful as you were, too. I can get myself another boy. So run along. Go back to your Mary Jane. Marry her, settle down, raise six kids and the payments for the mortgage. Sweat out the rest of your days in some lousy factory, rendering chicken-fat."

"Thanks." Luther smiled. "No hard feelings, then?" He moved towards the door, then halted. "Wait until I explain to Mary Jane!" he said. "You know, I almost had her convinced you were the Devil, too? I really believed the whole deal about how you had organized to ruin the world with rock-'n-roll and like that. Thanks for relieving my mind."

"Get lost," I said.

LUTHER SNODGRASS went out. Out of the door, out of my hair. I reached up and touched my hair as Judge Harmer came in.

"Well?" he asked.

"You must have heard his voice," I told him. "I can't use anything like that. Send in this new kid—this Randy Studd."

Judge Harmer hesitated.

"You mean you let Luther Snodgrass go? Just like that?"

"Why not? He's got everything figured out. I'm only a no-talent scout, in business for my wealth. No problem."

Judge Harmer nodded and made his exit.

I continued to touch my hair, brushing my hand over my head carefully, so as not to muss my toupee.

That toupee cost $2,000, but it's worth it.

It hides the horns...

THE END

If you've enjoyed this book, you will not want to miss these terrific titles...

ARMCHAIR SCI-FI, FANTASY, & HORROR DOUBLE NOVELS, $12.95 each

D-21   **EMPIRE OF EVIL** by Robert Arnette
            THE SIGN OF THE TIGER by Alan E. Nourse & J. A. Meyer

D-22   **OPERATION SQUARE PEG** by Frank Belknap Long
            ENCHANTRESS OF VENUS by Leigh Brackett

D-23   **THE LIFE WATCH** by Lester del Rey
            CREATURES OF THE ABYSS by Murray Leinster

D-24   **LEGION OF LAZARUS** by Edmond Hamilton
            STAR HUNTER by Andre Norton

D-25   **EMPIRE OF WOMEN** by John Fletcher
            ONE OF OUR CITIES IS MISSING by Irving Cox

D-26   **THE WRONG SIDE OF PARADISE** by Raymond F. Jones
            THE INVOLUNTARY IMMORTALS by Rog Phillips

D-27   **EARTH QUARTER** by Damon Knight
            ENVOY TO NEW WORLDS by Keith Laumer

D-28   **SLAVES TO THE METAL HORDE** by Milton Lesser
            HUNTERS OUT OF TIME by Joseph E. Kelleam

D-29   **RX JUPITER SAVE US** by Ward Moore
            BEWARE THE USURPERS by Geoff St. Reynard

D-30   **SECRET OF THE SERPENT** by Don Wilcox
            CRUSADE ACROSS THE VOID by Dwight V. Swain

ARMCHAIR SCIENCE FICTION CLASSICS, $12.95 each

C-7   **THE SHAVER MYSTERY, Book One**
            by Richard S. Shaver

C-8   **THE SHAVER MYSTERY, Book Two**
            by Richard S. Shaver

C-9   **MURDER IN SPACE** by David V. Reed
            by David V. Reed

ARMCHAIR MASTERS OF SCIENCE FICTION SERIES, $16.95 each

M-3   **MASTERS OF SCIENCE FICTION, Vol. Three**
            Robert Sheckley, "The Perfect Woman" and other tales

M-4   **MASTERS OF SCIENCE FICTION, Vol. Four**
            Mack Reynolds, "Stowaway" and other tales

If you've enjoyed this book, you will not want to miss these terrific titles...

ARMCHAIR SCI-FI & HORROR DOUBLE NOVELS, $12.95 each

D-31 **A HOAX IN TIME** by Keith Laumer
INSIDE EARTH by Poul Anderson

D-32 **TERROR STATION** by Dwight V. Swain
THE WEAPON FROM ETERNITY by Dwight V. Swain

D-33 **THE SHIP FROM INFINITY** by Edmond Hamilton
TAKEOFF by C. M. Kornbluth

D-34 **THE METAL DOOM** by David H. Keller
TWELVE TIMES ZERO by Howard Browne

D-35 **HUNTERS OUT OF SPACE** by Joseph Kelleam
INVASION FROM THE DEEP by Paul W. Fairman,

D-36 **THE BEES OF DEATH** by Robert Moore Williams
A PLAGUE OF PYTHONS by Frederick Pohl

D-37 **THE LORDS OF QUARMALL** by Fritz Leiber and Harry Fischer
BEACON TO ELSEWHERE by James H. Schmitz

D-38 **BEYOND PLUTO** by John S. Campbell
ARTERY OF FIRE by Thomas N. Scortia

D-39 **SPECIAL DELIVERY** by Kris Neville
NO TIME FOR TOFFEE by Charles F. Meyers

D-40 **JUNGLE IN THE SKY** by Milton Lesser
RECALLED TO LIFE by Robert Silverberg

ARMCHAIR SCIENCE FICTION CLASSICS, $12.95 each

C-10 **MARS IS MY DESTINATION**
by Frank Belknap Long

C-11 **SPACE PLAGUE**
by George O. Smith

C-12 **SO SHALL YE REAP**
by Rog Phillips

ARMCHAIR SCIENCE FICTION & HORROR GEMS SERIES, $12.95 each

G-3 **SCIENCE FICTION GEMS, Vol. Two**
James Blish and others

G-4 **HORROR GEMS, Vol. Two**
Joseph Payne Brennan and others

If you've enjoyed this book, you will not want to miss these terrific titles…

If you've enjoyed this book, you will not want to miss these terrific titles…

ARMCHAIR SCI-FI & HORROR DOUBLE NOVELS, $12.95 each

D-51 **A GOD NAMED SMITH** by Henry Slesar
WORLDS OF THE IMPERIUM by Keith Laumer

D-52 **CRAIG'S BOOK** by Don Wilcox
EDGE OF THE KNIFE by H. Beam Piper

D-53 **THE SHINING CITY** by Rena M. Vale
THE RED PLANET by Russ Winterbotham

D-54 **THE MAN WHO LIVED TWICE** by Rog Phillips
VALLEY OF THE CROEN by Lee Tarbell

D-55 **OPERATION DISASTER** by Milton Lesser
LAND OF THE DAMNED by Berkeley Livingston

D-56 **CAPTIVE OF THE CENTAURIANESS** by Poul Anderson
A PRINCESS OF MARS by Edgar Rice Burroughs

D-57 **THE NON-STATISTICAL MAN** by Raymond F. Jones
MISSION FROM MARS by Rick Conroy

D-58 **INTRUDERS FROM THE STARS** by Ross Rocklynne
FLIGHT OF THE STARLING by Chester S. Geier

D-59 **COSMIC SABOTEUR** by Frank M. Robinson
LOOK TO THE STARS by Willard Hawkins

D-60 **THE MOON IS HELL!** by John W. Campbell, Jr.
THE GREEN WORLD by Hal Clement

ARMCHAIR SCIENCE FICTION CLASSICS, $12.95 each

C-16 **THE SHAVER MYSTERY, Book Three**
by Richard S. Shaver

C-17 **THE PLANET STRAPPERS**
by Raymond Z. Gallun

C-18 **THE FOURTH "R"**
by George O. Smith

ARMCHAIR SCIENCE FICTION & HORROR GEMS SERIES, $12.95 each

G-5 **SCIENCE FICTION GEMS, Vol. Three**
C. M. Kornbluth and others

G-6 **HORROR GEMS, Vol. Three**
August Derleth and others

If you've enjoyed this book, you will not want to miss these terrific titles…

ARMCHAIR SCI-FI & HORROR DOUBLE NOVELS, $12.95 each

D-61   **THE MAN WHO STOPPED AT NOTHING** by Paul W. Fairman
       TEN FROM INFINITY by Ivar Jorgensen

D-62   **WORLDS WITHIN** by Rog Phillips
       THE SLAVE by C.M. Kornbluth

D-63   **SECRET OF THE BLACK PLANET** by Milton Lesser
       THE OUTCASTS OF SOLAR III by Emmett McDowell

D-64   **WEB OF THE WORLDS** by Harry Harrison and Katherine MacLean
       RULE GOLDEN by Damon Knight

D-65   **TEN TO THE STARS** by Raymond Z. Gallun
       THE CONQUERORS by David H. Keller, M. D.

D-66   **THE HORDE FROM INFINITY** by Dwight V. Swain
       THE DAY THE EARTH FROZE by Gerald Hatch

D-67   **THE WAR OF THE WORLDS** by H. G. Wells
       THE TIME MACHINE by H. G. Wells

D-68   **STARCOMBERS** by Edmond Hamilton
       THE YEAR WHEN STARDUST FELL by Raymond F. Jones

D-69   **HOCUS-POCUS UNIVERSE** by Jack Williamson
       QUEEN OF THE PANTHER WORLD by Berkeley Livingston

D-70   **BATTERING RAMS OF SPACE** by Don Wilcox
       DOOMSDAY WING by George H. Smith

ARMCHAIR SCIENCE FICTION & FANTASY CLASSICS, $12.95 each

C-19   **EMPIRE OF JEGGA**
       by David V. Reed

C-20   **THE TOMORROW PEOPLE**
       by Judith Merril

C-21   **THE MAN FROM YESTERDAY**
       by Howard Browne as by Lee Francis

C-22   **THE TIME TRADERS**
       by Andre Norton

C-23   **ISLANDS OF SPACE**
       by John W. Campbell

C-24   **THE GALAXY PRIMES**
       by E. E. "Doc" Smith

If you've enjoyed this book, you will not want to miss these terrific titles…

ARMCHAIR SCI-FI & HORROR DOUBLE NOVELS, $12.95 each

LIFE EXPECTANCY ON OMEGA WAS THREE YEARS

Barrent had been tried, convicted, and memory-washed on Earth—an Earth strangely altered and stratified by fear of the radical and the non-conformist.

Now he was serving his sentence on Omega—a prison planet walled by a ring of hovering guard-ships from which there was no escape.

Omega was a world of horror, a savage, ruthless way of life. But it was only a momentary ordeal, a prelude to a return to Earth and the subtle terrors of its own status civilization.

ABOUT ROBERT SHECKLEY

Robert Sheckley...

...was born New York in 1928 and raised in New Jersey. He joined the U.S. Army in 1946, spending most of his enlistment in Korea. After graduation from New York University in 1951, he worked on a variety of jobs before publishing his first genre stories: *Fear in the Night, Proof of the Pudding, Final Examination,* and *Warrior Race* to name a few. As his career quickly blossomed, Sheckley wrote countless short stories for science fiction magazines like *Galaxy* and *Amazing Stories.*

He soon forayed into novels and TV screenplays. And although he wrote over two dozen novels and short novels in his career (including some in the Star Trek series), Sheckley is largely remembered for his wonderful legacy of short stories. Famed sci-fi author Alan Dean Foster was known to have called Sheckley, "the best short story writer the field has produced."

Robert Sheckley passed away on Dec. 9th, 2005 at the age of 77.

THE STATUS CIVILIZATION

By
ROBERT SHECKLEY

ARMCHAIR FICTION
PO Box 4369, Medford, Oregon   97501-0168

*For more information about Armchair Books and products, visit our
website at…*

www.armchairfiction.com

Or email us at…

armchairfiction@yahoo.com

CHAPTER ONE

His return to consciousness was a slow and painful process. It was a journey in which he traversed all time. He dreamed. He rose through thick layers of sleep, out of the imaginary beginnings of all things. He lifted a pseudopod from primordial ooze, and the pseudopod was *him*. He became an amoeba which contained *his* essence; then a fish marked with his own peculiar individuality; then an ape unlike all other apes. And finally, he became a man.

What kind of man? Dimly he saw himself, faceless, a beamer gripped tight on one hand, a corpse at his feet. *That* kind of man.

He awoke, rubbed his eyes, and waited for further memories to come.

No memories came. Not even his name.

He sat up hastily and willed memory to return. When it didn't, he looked around, seeking in his surroundings some clue to his identity.

He was sitting on a bed in a small gray room. There was a closed door on one side. On the other, through a curtained alcove, he could see a tiny lavatory. Light came into the room from some hidden source, perhaps from the ceiling itself. The room had a bed and a single chair, and nothing else.

He held his chin in his hand and closed his eyes. He tried to catalogue all his knowledge, and the implications of that knowledge. He knew that he was a man, species Homo sapiens, an inhabitant of the planet Earth. He spoke a language which he knew was English. (Did that mean that there were other languages?) He knew the commonplace names for things: room, light, chair. He possessed in addition a limited amount of general knowledge. He knew that there were many important things which he did not know, which he once had known.

Something must have happened to me.

That something could have been worse. If it had gone a little further, he might have been left a mindless creature without a language, unaware of being human, of being a man, of being of Earth. A certain amount had been left to him.

But when he tried to think beyond the basic facts in his possession, he came to a dark and horror-filled area. *Do Not Enter.* Exploration into his own mind was as dangerous as a journey to—what? He couldn't find an analogue, though he suspected that many existed.

I must have been sick.

That was the only reasonable explanation. He was a man with the recollection of memories. He must at one time have had that priceless wealth of recall which now he could only deduce from the limited evidence at his disposal. At one time he must have had specific memories of birds, trees, friends, family, status, a wife perhaps. Now he could only theorize about them. Once he had been able to say, this is like, or, that reminds me of. Now nothing reminded him of anything, and things were only like themselves. He had lost his powers of contrast and comparison. He could no longer analyze the present in terms of the experienced past.

This must be a hospital.

Of course. He was being cared for in this place. Kindly doctors were working to restore his memory, to replace his identity, to restore his judgment apparatus, to tell him who and what he was. It was very good of them; he felt tears of gratitude start in his eyes.

He stood up and walked slowly around his small room. He went to the door and found it locked. That locked door gave him a moment of panic which he sternly controlled. Perhaps he had been violent.

Well, he wouldn't be violent any more. They'd see. They would award him all possible patient privileges. He would speak about that with the doctor.

He waited. After a long time, he heard footsteps coming down the corridor outside his door. He sat on the edge of the cot and listened, trying to control his excitement.

The footsteps stopped beside his door. A panel slid open, and a face peered in.

"How are you feeling?" the man asked.

He walked up to the panel, and saw that the man who questioned him was dressed in a brown uniform. He had an object on his waist which could be identified, after a moment, as a weapon. This man was undoubtedly a guard. He had a blunt, unreadable face.

"Could you tell me my name?" he asked the guard.

"Call yourself 402," the guard said. "That's your cell number."

He didn't like it. But 402 was better than nothing at all. He asked the guard, "Have I been sick for long? Am I getting better?"

"Yes," the guard said, in a voice that carried no conviction. "The important thing is, stay quiet. Obey the rules. That's the best way."

"Certainly," said 402. "But why can't I remember anything?"

"Well, that's the way it goes," the guard said. He started to walk away.

402 called after him, "Wait! You can't just leave me like this, you have to tell me something. What happened to me? Why am I in this hospital?"

"Hospital?" the guard said. He turned toward 402 and grinned. "What gave you the idea this was a hospital?"

"I assumed it," 402 said.

"You assumed wrong. This is a prison."

402 remembered his dream of the murdered man. Dream or memory? Desperately he called after the guard. "What was my offense? What did I do?"

"You'll find out," the guard said.

"When?"

"After we land," the guard said. "Now get ready for assembly."

He walked away. 402 sat down on the bed and tried to think. He had learned a few things. He was in a prison, and the prison was going to land. What did that mean? Why did a prison have to land? And what was an assembly?

402 had only a confused idea of what happened next. An unmeasurable amount of time passed. He was sitting on his bed, trying to piece together facts about himself. He had an impression of bells ringing. And then the door of his cell flew open.

Why was that? What did it mean?

402 walked to the door and peered into the corridor. He was very excited, but he didn't want to leave the security of his cell. He waited, and the guard came up.

"All right, now," the guard said, "No one's going to hurt you. Go straight down the corridor."

The guard pushed him gently. 402 walked down the corridor. He saw other cell doors opening, other men coming into the corridor. It was a thin stream at first; but as he continued walking, more and more men crowded into the passageway. Most of them looked bewildered, and none of them talked. The only words were from the guards:

"Move along now, keep on moving, straight ahead."

They were headed into a large circular auditorium. Looking around, 402 saw that a balcony ran around the room, and armed guards were stationed every few yards along it. Their presence seemed unnecessary; these cowed and bewildered men weren't going to stage a revolt. Still, he supposed the grim-faced guards had a symbolic value. They reminded the newly awakened men of the most important fact of their lives: that they were prisoners.

After a few minutes, a man in a somber uniform stepped out on the balcony. He held up his hand for attention, although the prisoners were already watching him fixedly. Then, though he had no visible means of amplification, his voice boomed hollowly through the auditorium.

"This is an indoctrination talk," he said. "Listen carefully and try to absorb what I am about to tell you. These facts will be very important for your existence."

The prisoners watched him. The speaker said, "All of you have, within the last hour, awakened in your cells. You have discovered that you cannot remember your former lives—not even your names. All you possess is a meager store of generalized knowledge; enough to keep you in touch with reality.

"I will not add to your knowledge. All of you, back on Earth, were vicious and depraved criminals. You were people of the worst sort, men who had forfeited any right to consideration by the State. In a less enlightened age, you would have been executed. In our age, you have been deported."

The speaker held out his hands to quiet the murmur that ran through the auditorium. He said, "All of you are criminals. And all of you have one thing in common: an inability to obey the basic obligatory rules of human society. Those rules are necessary for civilization to function. By disobeying them, you have committed crimes against all mankind. Therefore mankind rejects you. You are grit in the machinery of civilization, and you have been sent to a world where your own sort is king. Here you can make your own rules, and die by them. Here is the freedom you lusted for; the uncontained and self-destroying freedom of a cancerous growth."

The speaker wiped his forehead and glared earnestly at the prisoners. "But perhaps," he said, "a rehabilitation is possible for some of you. Omega, the planet to which we are going, is *your* planet, a place ruled entirely by prisoners. It is a world where you could begin again, with no prejudices against you, with a clean record! Your past lives are forgotten. Don't try to remember them. Such memories would serve only to restimulate your criminal tendencies. Consider yourselves born afresh as of the moment of awakening in your cells."

The speaker's slow, measured words had a certain hypnotic quality. 402 listened, his eyes slightly unfocused and fixed upon the speaker's pale forehead.

"A new world," the speaker was saying. "You are reborn—but with the necessary consciousness of sin. Without it, you would be unable to combat the evil inherent in your personalities. Remember that. Remember that there is no escape and no return. Guardships armed with the latest beam weapons patrol the skies of Omega day and night. These ships are designed to obliterate anything that rises more than five hundred feet above the surface of the planet—an invincible barrier through which no prisoner can ever pass. Accommodate yourselves to these facts. They constitute the rules which must govern your lives. Think about what I've said. And now stand by for landing."

The speaker left the balcony. For a while, the prisoners simply stared at the spot where he had been. Then, tentatively, a murmur of conversation began. After a while it died away. There was nothing to talk about. The prisoners, without memory of the past, had nothing upon which to base a speculation of the future. Personalities could not be exchanged, for those personalities were newly emerged and still undefined.

They sat in silence, uncommunicative men who had been too long in solitary confinement. The guards on the balcony stood like statues, remote and impersonal. And then the faintest tremor ran through the floor of the auditorium.

The tremor came again; then it changed into a definite vibration. 402 felt heavier, as though an invisible weight were pressing against his head and shoulders.

A loudspeaker voice called out, "Attention! The ship is now landing on Omega. We will disembark shortly."

The last vibration died away, and the floor beneath them gave a slight lurch. The prisoners, still silent and dazed, were formed into a long line and marched out of the auditorium. Flanked by guards, they went down a corridor which stretched on interminably. From it, 402 began to get some idea of the size of the ship.

Far ahead, he could see a patch of sunlight which shone brightly against the pale illumination of the corridor. His section of the long shuffling line reached the sunlight, and 402 saw that it came from an open hatchway through which the prisoners were passing.

In his turn, 402 went through the hatchway, climbed down a long stairway, and found himself on solid ground. He was standing in an open, sunlit square. Guards were forming the disembarked prisoners into files; on all sides, 402 could see a crowd of spectators watching.

A loudspeaker voice boomed, "Answer when your number is called. Your identity will now be revealed to you. Answer promptly when your number is called."

402 felt weak and very tired. Not even his identity could interest him now. All he wanted to do was lie down, to sleep, to have a chance to think about his situation. He looked around and took casual note of the huge starcraft behind him, of the guards, the spectators. Overhead, he saw black dots moving against a blue sky. At first he thought they were birds. Then, looking closer, he saw they were guardships. He wasn't particularly interested in them.

"Number 1! Speak out!"

"Here," a voice answered.

"Number 1, your name is Wayn Southholder. Age 34, blood type A-L2, Index AR-431-C. Guilty of treason."

When the voice had finished, a loud cheer came up from the crowd. They were applauding the prisoner's traitorous actions, and welcoming him to Omega.

The names were read down the list, and 402, drowsy in the sunshine, dozed on his feet and listened to the crimes of murder, credit theft, deviationalism, and mutantism. At last his number was called.

"Number 402."

"Here."

"Number 402, your name is Will Barrent. Age 27, blood type O-L3, Index JX-221-R. Guilty of murder."

The crowd cheered, but 402 scarcely heard them. He was trying to accustom himself to the idea of having a name. A real name instead of a number. Will Barrent. He hoped he wouldn't forget it. He repeated the name to himself over and over again, and almost missed the last announcement from the ship's loudspeaker.

"The new men are now released upon Omega. You will be given temporary housing at Square A-2. Be cautious and circumspect in your words and actions. Watch, listen, and learn. The law requires me to tell you that the average life expectancy on Omega is approximately three Earth years."

It took a while for those last words to take effect on Barrent. He was still contemplating the novelty of having a name. He hadn't considered any of the implications of being a murderer on an underworld planet.

CHAPTER TWO

The new prisoners were led to a row of barracks at Square A-2. There were nearly five hundred of them. They were not yet men; they were entities whose true memories extended barely an hour in time. Sitting on their bunks, the newborns looked curiously at their bodies, examined with sharp interest their hands and feet. They stared at each other, and saw their formlessness mirrored in each other's eyes. They were not yet men; but they were not children either. Certain abstractions remained, and the ghosts of memories. Maturation came quickly, born of old habit patterns and personality traits, retained in the broken threads of their former lives on Earth.

The new men clung to the vague recollections of concepts, ideas, rules. Within a few hours, their phlegmatic blandness had begun to pass. They were becoming men now. Individuals. Out of a dazed and superficial conformity, sharp differences began to emerge. Character reasserted itself, and the five hundred began to discover what they were.

Will Barrent stood in line for a look at himself in the barracks mirror. When his turn came, he saw the reflection of a thin-faced, narrow-nosed, pleasant-looking young man with straight brown hair. The young man had a resolute, honest, unexceptional face, unmarked by any strong passion. Barrent turned away disappointed; it was the face of a stranger.

Later, examining himself more closely, he could find no scars or anything else to distinguish his body from a thousand other bodies. His hands were uncalloused. He was wiry rather than muscular. He wondered what sort of work he had done on Earth.

Murder?

He frowned. He wasn't ready to accept that.

A man tapped him on the shoulder. "How you feeling?"

Barrent turned and saw a large, thick-shouldered red-haired man standing beside him.

"Pretty good," Barrent said. "You were in line behind me, weren't you?"

"That's right. Number 401. Name's Danis Foeren."

Barrent introduced himself.

"Your crime?" Foeren asked.

"Murder."

Foeren nodded, looking impressed. "Me, I'm a forger. Wouldn't think it to look at my hands." He held out two massive paws covered with sparse red hair. "But the skill's there. My hands remembered before any other part of me. On the ship I sat in my cell and looked at my hands. They itched. They wanted to be off and doing things. But the rest of me couldn't remember what."

"What did you do?" Barrent asked.

"I closed my eyes and let my hands take over," Foeren said. "First thing I knew, they were up and picking the lock of the cell." He held up his huge hands and looked at them admiringly. "Clever little devils!"

"Picking the lock?" Barrent asked. "But I thought you were a forger."

"Well, now," Foeren said, "forgery was my main line. But a pair of skilled hands can do almost anything. I suspect that I was only *caught* for forgery; but I might also have been a safeman. My hands know too much for just a forger."

"You've found out more about yourself than I have," Barrent said. "All I have to start with is a dream."

"Well, that's a start," Foeren said. "There must be ways of finding out more. The important thing is, we're on Omega."

"Agreed," Barrent said sourly.

"Nothing wrong with that," Foeren said. "Didn't you hear what the man said? This is our planet!"

"With an average life expectancy of three Earth years," Barrent reminded him.

"That's probably just scare talk," Foeren said. "I wouldn't believe stuff like that from a guard. The big thing is, we have our own planet. You heard what they said. 'Earth rejects us.' Nova Earth! Who needs her? We've our own planet here. A whole planet, Barrent! We're free!"

Another man said, "That's right, friend." He was small, furtive-eyed, and ingratiatingly friendly. "My name is Joe," he told them. "Actually, the name is Joao; but I prefer the archaic form with its flavor of more gracious times. Gentlemen, I couldn't help overhearing your conversation, and I agree most heartily with our red-haired friend. Consider the possibilities! Earth has cast us aside? Excellent! We are better off without her. We are all equal here, free men in a free society. No uniforms, no guards, no soldiers. Just repentant former criminals who want to live in peace."

"What did they get you for?" Barrent asked.

"They said I was a credit thief," Joe said. "I'm ashamed to admit that I can't remember what a credit thief is. But perhaps it'll come back to me."

"Maybe the authorities have some sort of memory retraining system," Foeren said.

"Authorities?" Joe said indignantly. "What do you mean, authorities? This is *our* planet. We're all equal here. By definition, there can't be any authorities. No, friends, we left all that nonsense behind on Earth. Here we—"

He stopped abruptly. The barracks' door had opened and a man walked in. He was evidently an older resident of Omega since he lacked the gray prison uniform. He was fat, and dressed in garish yellow and blue clothing. On a belt around his ample waist he carried a holstered pistol and a knife. He stood just inside the doorway, his hands on his hips, glaring at the new arrivals.

"Well?" he said. "Don't you new men recognize a Quaestor? Stand up!"

None of the men moved.

The Quaestor's face went scarlet. "I guess I'll have to teach you a little respect."

Even before he had taken his weapon from its holster, the new arrivals had scrambled to their feet. The Quaestor looked at them with a faintly regretful air and pushed the weapon back in its holster.

"The first thing you men better learn," the Quaestor said, "is your status on Omega. Your status is *nowhere*. You're peons, and that means you're *nothing*."

He waited a moment and then said, "Now pay attention, peons. You are about to be instructed in your duties."

CHAPTER THREE

"The first thing you new men should understand," the Quaestor said, "is just exactly what you are. That's very important. And I'll tell you what you are. You're *peons*. You're the lowest of the low. You're *statusless*. There's nothing lower except mutants, and they aren't really human. Any questions?"

The Quaestor waited. When there were no questions, he said, "I've defined what *you* are. From that, we'll proceed to a basic understanding of what everybody else on Omega is. First of all, *everybody* is more important than you; but some are more important than others. Next above you in rank is the Resident, who hardly counts for more than any of you, and then there's the Free Citizen. He wears a gray finger ring of status, and his clothes are black. He isn't important either, but he's much more important than you. With luck, some of you may become Free Citizens.

"Next are the Privileged Classes, all distinguished by various recognition symbols according to rank—such as the golden earrings, for example, of the Hadji class. Eventually you'll learn all the marks and prerogatives of the various ranks and degrees. I might also mention the priests. Even though they're not of Privileged rank, they're granted certain immunities and rights. Have I made myself clear?"

Everyone in the barracks mumbled assent. The Quaestor continued, "Now we come to the subject of deportment when meeting anyone of superior rank. As peons, you are obliged to greet a Free Citizen by his full title, in a respectful manner. With Privileged ranks such as Hadjis you speak only when spoken to, and then you stand with eyes downcast and hands clasped in front of you. You do not leave the presence of a Privileged Citizen until permission has been granted. You do not sit in his company under any circumstances. Understood? There is much more to be learned. My office of Quaestor, for example, comes under the classification of Free Citizen, but carries certain of the prerogatives of Privilege."

The Quaestor glared at the men to make sure they understood. "This barracks is your temporary home. I have drawn up a chart to show which men sweep, which wash, and so forth. You may question me at anytime; but foolish or impertinent questions can be punished by mutilation or death. Just remember that you are the lowest of the low. If you bear that in mind, you might be able to stay alive."

The Quaestor stood in silence for a few moments. Then he said, "Over the next few days, you'll all be given various assignments. Some of you will go to the germanium mines, some to the fishing fleet, some will be apprenticed to various trades. In the meantime, you're free to look around Tetrahyde."

When the men looked blank, the Quaestor explained, "Tetrahyde is the name of the city you're in. It's the largest city on Omega." He thought for a moment. "In fact, it's the only city on Omega."

"What does the name Tetrahyde mean?" Joe asked.

"How should I know?" the Quaestor said, scowling. "I suppose it's one of those old Earth names the skrenners are always coming up with. Anyhow, just watch your step when you enter it."

"Why?" Barrent asked.

The Quaestor grinned. "That, peon, is something you'll have to find out for yourself." He turned and strode from the barracks.

When he had gone, Barrent went to the window. From it he could see a deserted square and, beyond, the streets of Tetrahyde.

"You thinking of going out there?" Joe asked.

"Certainly I am," Barrent said. "Coming with me?"

The little credit thief shook his head. "I don't think it's safe."

"Foeren, how about you?"

"I don't like it either," Foeren said. "Might be better to stay around the barracks for a while."

"That's ridiculous," Barrent said. "It's *our* city now. Isn't anyone coming with me?"

Looking uncomfortable, Foeren hunched his big shoulders and shook his head. Joe shrugged and lay back on his cot. The rest of the new men didn't even look up.

"Very well," Barrent said. "I'll give you a full report later." He waited a moment longer in case someone changed his mind, then went out the door.

THE CITY of Tetrahyde was a collection of buildings sprawled along a narrow peninsula which jutted into a sluggish gray sea. The peninsula's landward side was contained by a high stone wall, pierced with gates and guarded by sentries. Its largest building was the Arena, used once a year for the Games. Near the Arena was a small cluster of government buildings.

Barrent walked along the narrow streets, staring around him, trying to get some idea of what his new home was like. The winding, unpaved roads and dark, weatherbeaten houses stirred an elusive tag-end of memory in him. He had seen a place like this on Earth, but he couldn't remember anything about it. The recollection was as tantalizing as an itch; but he couldn't locate its source.

Past the Arena, he came into the main business district of Tetrahyde. Fascinated, he read the store signs: UNLICENSED DOCTOR—ABORTIONS PERFORMED WHILE-U-WAIT. Further on, DISBARRED LAWYER. POLITICAL PULL!

This seemed vaguely wrong to Barrent. He walked further, past stores advertising stolen goods, past a little shop that announced: MIND READING! FULL STAFF OF SKRENNING MUTANTS! YOUR PAST ON EARTH REVEALED!

Barrent was tempted to go in. But he remembered that he hadn't any money; and Omega seemed like the sort of place that put a high value on money.

He turned down a side street, walked by several restaurants, and came to a large building called THE POISON INSTITUTE (*Easy Terms. Up to 3 Years to Pay. Satisfaction Guaranteed or Your Money Back*). Next door to it was THE ASSASSIN'S GUILD, *Local 452.*

On the basis of the indoctrination talk on the prison ship, Barrent had expected Omega to be dedicated to the rehabilitation of criminals. To judge by the store signs, this simply wasn't so; or if it was, rehabilitation took some very strange forms. He walked on more slowly, deep in thought.

Then he noticed that people were moving out of his way. They glanced at him and ducked in doorways and stores. An elderly woman took one look at him and ran.

What was wrong? Could it be his prison uniform? No, the people of Omega had seen many of those. What was it, then?

The street was almost deserted. A shopkeeper near him was hurriedly swinging steel shutters over his display of fencing equipment.

"What's the matter?" Barrent asked him. "What's going on?"

"Are you out of your head?" the shopkeeper said. "It's Landing Day!"

"I beg your pardon?"

"Landing Day!" the shopkeeper said. "The day the prison ship landed. Get back to your barracks, you idiot!"

He slammed the last steel shutter into place and locked it. Barrent felt a sudden cold touch of fear. Something was very wrong. He had better get back in a hurry. It had been stupid of him not to find out more about Omegan customs before...

Three men were walking down the street toward him. They were well dressed, and each wore the small golden Hadji earring in his left ear. All three men carried sidearms.

Barrent started to walk away from them. One of the men shouted, "Stop, peon!"

Barrent saw that the man's hand was dangling near his gun. He stopped and said, "What's the matter?"

"It's Landing Day," the man said. He looked at his friends. "Well, who gets him first?"

"We'll choose."

"Here's a coin."

"No, a show of fingers."

"Ready? One, two, three!"

"He's mine," said the Hadji on the left. His friends moved back as he drew his sidearm.

"Wait!" Barrent called out. "What are you doing?"

"I'm going to shoot you," the man said.

"But why?"

The man smiled. "Because it's a Hadji privilege. On every Landing Day, we have the right to shoot down any new peon who leaves his barracks area."

"But I wasn't told!"

"Of course not," the man said. "If you new men were told, none of you would leave your barracks on Landing Day. And that would spoil all the fun."

He took aim.

Barrent reacted instantaneously. He threw himself to the ground as the Hadji fired, heard a hiss, and saw a jagged heatburn score the brick building next to which he had been standing.

"My turn now," one of the men said.

"Sorry, old man, I believe it's mine."

"Seniority, dear friend, has its privileges. Stand clear."

Before the next man could take aim, Barrent was on his feet and running. The sharply winding street protected him for the moment, but he could hear the sounds of his pursuers behind him. They were running at an easy stride, almost a fast walk, as if they were completely sure of their prey. Barrent put on a burst of speed, turned down a side street, and knew immediately he had made a mistake. He was facing a dead end. The Hadjis, moving at an easy pace, were coming up behind him.

Barrent looked wildly around. Store fronts here were all locked and shuttered. There was nowhere he could climb to, no place to hide.

And then he saw an open door halfway down the block in the direction of his pursuers. He had run right by it. A sign protruding from the building above the doorway said THE VICTIM'S PROTECTIVE SOCIETY. That's for me, Barrent thought.

He sprinted for it, running almost under the noses of the startled Hadjis. A single gun blast scorched the ground under his heels; then he had reached the doorway and flung himself inside.

He scrambled to his feet. His pursuers had not followed him; he could still hear their voices in the street, amiably arguing questions of precedence. Barrent realized he had entered some sort of sanctuary.

He was in a large, brightly lighted room. Several ragged men were sitting on a bench near the door, laughing at a private joke. A little further down, a dark-haired girl sat and watched Barrent with wide, unblinking green eyes. At the far end of the room was a desk with a man sitting behind it. The man beckoned to Barrent.

He walked up to the desk. The man behind it was short and bespectacled. He smiled encouragingly, waiting for Barrent to speak.

"This is the Victim's Protective Society?" Barrent asked.

"Quite correct, sir," the man said. "I am Rondolp Frendlyer, president of this nonprofit organization. Could I be of service?"

"You certainly could," Barrent said. "I'm practically a victim."

"I knew that just by looking at you," Frendlyer said, smiling warmly. "You have a certain *victim* look; a mixture of fear and uncertainty with just a suggestion of vulnerability thrown in. It's quite unmistakable."

"That's very interesting," Barrent said, glancing toward the door and wondering how long his sanctuary would be respected. "Mr. Frendlyer, I'm not a member of your organization—"

"That doesn't matter," Frendlyer said. "Membership in our group is necessarily spontaneous. One joins when the occasion arises. Our intention is to protect the inalienable rights of all victims."

"Yes, sir. Well, there are three men outside trying to kill me."

"I see," Mr. Frendlyer said. He opened a drawer and took out a large book. He flipped through it quickly and found the reference he wanted. "Tell me, did you ascertain the status of these men?"

"I believe they were Hadjis," Barrent said. "Each of them had a little gold earring in his left ear."

"Quite right," Mr. Frendlyer said. "And today is Landing Day. You came off the ship that landed today, and have been classified a peon. Is that correct?"

"Yes, it is," Barrent said.

"Then I'm happy to say that everything is in order. The Landing Day Hunt ends at sundown. You can leave here with knowledge that everything is correct and that your rights are in no way being violated."

"Leave here? After sundown, you mean."

Mr. Frendlyer shook his head and smiled sadly. "I'm afraid not. According to the law, you must leave here at once."

"But they'll kill me!"

"That's very true," Frendlyer said. "Unfortunately, it can't be helped. A victim, by definition, is one who is to be killed."

"I thought this was a protective organization."

"It is. But we protect *rights*, not victims. Your rights are not being violated. The Hadjis have the privilege of killing you on Landing Day, at any time before sundown, if you are not in your barracks area. You, I might add, have the right to kill anyone who tries to kill you."

"I don't have a weapon," Barrent said.

"Victims never do," Frendlyer said. "It makes all the difference, doesn't it? But weapon or not, I'm afraid you'll have to leave now."

Barrent could still hear the Hadjis' lazy voices in the street. He asked, "Have you a rear door?"

"Sorry."

"Then I'll simply not leave."

Still smiling, Mr. Frendlyer opened a drawer and took out a gun. He pointed it at Barrent, and said, "You really must leave. You can take your chances with the Hadjis, or you can die right here with no chance at all."

"Lend me your gun," Barrent said.

"It isn't allowed," Frendlyer told him. "Can't have victims running around with weapons, you know. It would upset things." He clicked off the safety. "Are you leaving?"

Barrent calculated his chances of diving across the desk for the gun, and decided he would never make it. He turned and walked slowly to the door. The ragged men were still laughing together. The dark-haired girl had risen from the bench and was standing near the doorway. As he came close to her, Barrent noticed that she was very lovely. He wondered what crime had dictated her expulsion from Earth.

As he passed her, he felt something hard pressed into his ribs. He reached for it, and found he was holding a small, efficient-looking gun.

"Luck," the girl said. "I hope you know how to use it."

Barrent nodded his thanks. He wasn't sure he knew how; but he was going to find out.

CHAPTER FOUR

The street was deserted except for the three Hadjis, who stood about twenty yards away, conversing quietly. As Barrent came through the doorway, two of the men moved back; the third, his sidearm negligently lowered, stepped forward. When he saw that Barrent was armed he quickly brought his gun into firing position.

Barrent flung himself to the ground and pressed the trigger of his unfamiliar weapon. He felt it vibrate in his hand, and saw the Hadji's head and shoulders turn black and begin to crumble. Before he could take aim at the other men, Barrent's gun was wrenched violently from his hand. The Hadji's dying shot had creased the end of the muzzle.

Desperately Barrent dived for the gun, knowing he could never reach it in time. His skin pricked in expectation of the killing shot. He rolled to his gun, still miraculously alive, and took aim at the nearest Hadji.

Just in time, he checked himself from firing. The Hadjis had holstered their weapons. One of them was saying, "Poor old Draken. He simply could not learn to take quick aim."

"Lack of practice," the other man said. "Draken never spent much time on the firing range."

"Well, if you ask me, it's a very good object lesson. One mustn't get out of practice."

"And," the other man said, "one mustn't underestimate even a peon." He looked at Barrent. "Nice shooting, fellow."

"Yes, very nice indeed," the other man said. "It's difficult to fire a handgun accurately while in motion."

Barrent got to his feet shakily, still holding the girl's weapon, prepared to fire at the first suspicious movement from the Hadjis. But they weren't moving suspiciously. They seemed to regard the entire incident as closed.

"What happens now?" Barrent asked.

"Nothing," one of the Hadjis said. "On Landing Day, one kill is all that any man or hunting party is allowed. After that, you're out of the hunt."

"It's really a very unimportant holiday," the other man said. "Not like the Games or the Lottery."

"All that remains for you to do," the first man said, "is to go to the Registration Office and collect your inheritance."

"My *what*?"

"Your inheritance," the Hadji said patiently. "You're entitled to the entire estate of your victim. In Draken's case, I'm sorry to say, it doesn't amount to very much."

"He never was a good businessman," the other said sadly. "Still, it'll give you a little something to start life with. And since you've made an authorized kill—even though a highly unusual one—you move upward in status. You become a Free Citizen."

People had come back into the streets, and shopkeepers were unlocking their steel shutters. A truck marked BODY DISPOSAL UNIT 5 drove up, and four uniformed men took away Draken's body. The normal life of Tetrahyde had begun again. This, more than any assurances from the Hadjis, told Barrent that the moment for murder was over. He put the girl's weapon in his pocket.

"The Registration Office is over this way," one of the Hadjis told him. "We'll act as your witnesses."

Barrent still had only a limited understanding of the situation. But since things were suddenly going his way, he decided to accept whatever happened without question. There would be plenty of time later to find out where he stood.

Accompanied by the Hadjis, he went to the Registration Office on Gunpoint Square. There a bored clerk heard the entire story, produced Draken's business papers, and pasted Barrent's name over Draken's. Barrent noticed that several other names had been pasted over. There seemed to be a fast turnover of businesses in Tetrahyde.

He found that he was now the owner of an antidote shop at 3 Blazer Boulevard.

The business papers also officially recognized Barrent's new rank as a Free Citizen. The clerk gave him a ring of status, made of gunmetal, and advised him to change into Citizen's clothing as soon as possible if he wished to avoid unpleasant incidents.

Outside, the Hadjis wished him luck. Barrent decided to see what his new business was like.

BLAZER BOULEVARD was a short alley running between two streets. Near the middle of it was a store front with a sign which read: ANTIDOTE SHOP. Beneath that it read: *Specifics for every poison, whether animal, vegetable, or mineral. Carry our handy Do It Yourself Survival Kit. Twenty-three antidotes in one pocket-sized container!*

Barrent opened the door and went in. Behind a low counter he saw ceiling-high shelves stocked with labeled bottles, cans and cartons, and square glass jars containing odd bits of leaves, twigs, and fungus. In back of the counter was a small shelf of books with titles like *Quick Diagnosis in Acute Poisoning Cases*; *The Arsenic Family*; and *The Permutations of Henbane*.

It was quite obvious that poisoning played a large part in the daily life of Omega. Here was a store—and presumably there were others—whose sole purpose was to dispense antidotes. Barrent thought about this and decided that he had inherited a strange but honorable business. He would study the books and find out how an antidote shop was run.

The store had a back apartment with a living room, bedroom, and kitchen. In one of the closets, Barrent found a badly made suit of Citizen black, into which he changed. He took the girl's weapon from the pocket of his prison ship uniform, weighed it in his hand for a moment, then put it into a pocket of his new suit. He left the store and found his way back to the Victim's Protective Society.

The door was still open, and the three ragged men were still sitting on the bench. They weren't laughing now. Their long wait seemed to have tired them. At the other end of the room, Mr. Frendlyer was seated behind his desk, reading through a thick pile of papers. There was no sign of the girl.

Barrent walked to the desk, and Frendlyer stood up to greet him.

"My congratulations!" Frendlyer said. "Dear fellow, my very warmest congratulations. That was a splendid bit of shooting. And in motion, too!"

"Thank you," Barrent said. "The reason I came back here—"

"I know why," Frendlyer said. "You wished to be advised of your rights and obligations as a Free Citizen. What could be more natural? If you take a seat on that bench, I'll be with you in—"

"I didn't come here for that," Barrent said. "I want to find out about my rights and obligations, of course. But right now, I want to find that girl."

"Girl?"

"She was sitting on the bench when I came in. She was the one who gave me the gun."

Mr. Frendlyer looked astonished. "Citizen, you must be laboring under a misapprehension. There has been no woman in this office all day."

"She was sitting on the bench near those three men. A very attractive dark-haired girl. You must have noticed her."

"I would certainly have noticed her if she had been here," Frendlyer said, winking. "But as I said before, no woman has entered these premises today."

Barrent glared at him and pulled the gun out of his pocket. "In that case, how did I get this?"

"I lent it to you," Frendlyer said. "I'm glad you were able to use it successfully, but now I would appreciate its return."

"You're lying," Barrent said, taking a firm grip on the weapon. "Let's ask those men."

He walked over to the bench with Frendlyer close behind him. He caught the attention of the man who had been sitting nearest the girl and asked him, "Where did the girl go?"

The man lifted a sullen, unshaven face and said, "What girl you talking about, Citizen?"

"The one who was sitting right here."

"I didn't notice nobody. Rafeel, you see a female on this bench?"

"Not me," Rafeel said. "And I been sitting here continuous since ten this morning."

"I didn't see her neither," the third man said. "And I got sharp eyes."

Barrent turned back to Frendlyer. "Why are you lying to me?"

"I've told you the simple truth," Frendlyer said. "There has been no girl in here all day. I lent you the gun, as is my privilege as President of the Victim's Protective Society. I would now appreciate its return."

"No," Barrent said. "I'm keeping the gun until I find the girl."

"That might not be wise," Frendlyer said. He hastily added, "Thievery, I mean, is not condoned under these circumstances."

"I'll take my chances on that," Barrent said. He turned and left the Victim's Protective Society.

CHAPTER FIVE

Barrent needed time to recuperate from his violent entry into Omegan life. Starting from the helpless state of a newborn, he had moved through murder to the ownership of an antidote shop. From a forgotten past on a planet called Earth, he had been catapulted into a dubious present in a world full of criminals. He had gotten a glimpse of a complex class structure, and a hint of an institutionalized program of murder. He had discovered in himself a certain measure of self-reliance, and a surprising quickness with a gun. He knew there was a great deal more to find out about Omega, Earth, and himself. He hoped he would live long enough to make the necessary discoveries.

First things first. He had to earn a living. To do so, he had to find out about poisons and antidotes.

He moved into the apartment in back of his store and began reading the books left by the late Hadji Draken.

The literature on poisons was fascinating. There were the vegetable poisons known on Earth, such as hellebore, setterwort, deadly nightshade, and the yew tree. He learned about the action of hemlock—its preliminary intoxication and its final convulsions. There was prussic acid poisoning from almonds and digitalin poisoning from purple foxglove. There was the awesome efficiency of wolfsbane with its deadly store of aconite. There were the fungi such as the amanita toadstools and fly agaric, not to mention the purely Omegan vegetable poisons like redcup, flowering lily, and amortalis.

But the vegetable poisons, although dismayingly numerous, were only one part of his studies. He had to consider the animals of Earth, sea, and air, the several species of deadly spiders, the snakes, scorpions, and giant wasps. There was an imposing array of metallic poisons such as arsenic, mercury, and bismuth. There were the commoner corrosives—nitric, hydrochloric, phosphoric, and sulphuric acid. And there were the poisons distilled or extracted from various sources, among which were strychnine, formic acid, hyoscyamine, and belladonna.

Each of the poisons had one or more antidotes listed; but those complicated, cautiously worded formulas, Barrent suspected, were frequently unsuccessful. To make matters more difficult, the efficacy of an antidote seemed to depend upon a correct diagnosis of the poisoning agent. And too often the symptoms produced by one poison resembled those of another.

Barrent pondered these problems while he studied his books. In the meantime, with considerable nervousness, he served his first customers.

He found that many of his fears were ungrounded. In spite of the dozens of lethal substances recommended by the Poison Institute, most poisoners stuck single-mindedly to arsenic or strychnine. They were cheap, sure, and very painful. Prussic acid had a readily discernible odor, mercury was difficult to introduce into the system, and the corrosives, although gratifyingly spectacular, were dangerous to the user. Wolfsbane and fly agaric were excellent, of course; deadly nightshade could not be discounted, and the amanita toadstool had its own macabre charm. But these were the poisons of an older, more leisurely age. The impatient younger generation—and especially the women, who made up nearly 90 per cent of the poisoners on Omega—were satisfied with plain arsenic or strychnine, as the occasion and opportunity demanded.

Omegan women were conservatives. They simply weren't interested in the never-ending refinements of the poisoner's art. Means didn't interest them; only ends, as quickly and as cheaply as possible. Omegan women were noted for their common sense. Although the eager theoreticians at the Poison Institute tried to sell dubious mixtures of Contact Poison or Three Day Mold, and worked hard to put across complex, haywire schemes involving wasps, concealed needles, and double glasses, they found few takers among women. Simple arsenic and fast-acting strychnine continued to be the mainstays of the poison trade.

This quite naturally simplified Barrent's work. His remedies—immediate regurgitation, lavage, neutralizing agent—were easy enough to master.

He encountered some difficulty with men who refused to believe they had been poisoned by anything so commonplace as arsenic or strychnine. For those cases, Barrent prescribed a variety of roots, herbs, twigs, leaves, and a minute homeopathic dose of poison. But he invariably preceded these with regurgitation, lavage, and neutralizing agent.

After he was settled, Barrent received a visit from Danis Foeren and Joe. Foeren had a temporary job on the docks unloading fishing boats. Joe had organized a nightly pokra game among the government workers of Tetrahyde. Neither man had moved much in status; with no kills to their credit, they had progressed only as far as Second Class Resident. They were nervous about meeting socially with a Free Citizen, but Barrent put them at ease. They were the only friends he had on Omega, and he had no intention of losing them over a question of social position.

Barrent was unable to learn very much from them about the laws and customs of Tetrahyde. Even Joe hadn't been able to find out anything definite from his friends in government service. On Omega, the law was kept secret. Older residents used their knowledge of the law to enforce their rule over the newcomers. This system was condoned and reinforced by the doctrine of the inequality of all men, which lay at the heart of the Omegan legal system. Through planned inequality and enforced ignorance, power and status remained in the hands of the older residents.

Of course, all social movement upward couldn't be stopped. But it could be retarded, discouraged, and made exceedingly dangerous. The way one encountered the laws and customs of Omega was through a risky process of trial and error.

Although the Antidote Shop took up most of his time, Barrent persisted in his efforts to locate the girl. He was unable to find a hint that she even existed.

He became friendly with the shopkeepers on either side of him. One of them, Demond Harrisbourg, was a jaunty, moustached young man who operated a food store. It was a mundane and slightly ridiculous line of work; but, as Harrisbourg explained, even criminals must eat. And this necessitated farmers, processors, packagers, and food stores. Harrisbourg contended that his business was in no way inferior to the more indigenous Omegan industries centered around violent death. Besides, Harrisbourg's wife's uncle was a Minister of Public Works. Through him, Harrisbourg expected to receive a murder certificate. With this all-important document, he could make his six-months kill and move upward to the status of Privileged Citizen.

Barrent nodded his agreement. But he wondered if Harrisbourg's wife, a thin, restless woman, wouldn't decide to poison him first. She appeared to be dissatisfied with her husband; and divorce was forbidden on Omega.

His other neighbor, Tem Rend, was a lanky, cheerful man in his early forties. He had a heat scar which ran from just beneath his left ear down almost to the corner of his mouth, a souvenir given him by a status-seeking hopeful. The hopeful had picked on the wrong man. Tem Rend owned a weapon shop, practiced constantly, and always carried the articles of his trade with him. According to witnesses, he had performed the counterkill in exemplary fashion. Tem's dream was to become a member of the Assassin's Guild. His application was on file with that ancient and austere organization, and he had a chance of being accepted within the month.

Barrent bought a sidearm from him. On Rend's advice, he chose a Jamiason-Tyre needlebeam. It was faster and more accurate than any projectile weapon, and it transmitted the same shock-power as a heavy caliber bullet. To be sure, it hadn't the spread of heat weapons such as the Hadjis used, which could kill within six inches of their target. But wide-range beamers encouraged inaccuracy. They were messy, careless weapons which reinforced careless traits. Anyone could fire a heat gun;

but to use a needlebeam effectively, you had to practice constantly. And practice paid off. A good needlebeam man was more than a match for any two widebeam gunmen.

Barrent took this advice to heart, coming, as it did, from an apprentice assassin and the owner of a weapon shop. He put in long hours on Rend's cellar firing range, sharpening his reflexes, getting used to the Quik-Thro holster.

There was a lot to do and a tremendous amount to learn, just in order to survive. Barrent didn't mind hard work as long as it was for a worthwhile goal. He hoped things would stay quiet for a while so he could catch up to the older inhabitants.

But things never stayed quiet in Omega.

One day, late in the afternoon as he was closing up, Barrent received an unusual-looking caller. He was a man in his fifties, heavy-set, with a stern, swarthy face. He wore a red ankle-length robe and sandals. Around his waist was a rawhide belt from which dangled a small black book and a red-handled dagger. There was an air of unusual force and authority about him. Barrent was unable to tell his status.

Barrent said, "I was just closing up, sir. But if there's anything you wish to buy—"

"I did not come here to buy," the caller said. He permitted himself a faint smile. "I came here to sell."

"Sell?"

"I am a priest," the man said. "You are a newcomer to my district. I haven't noticed you at services."

"I hadn't known anything about—"

The priest held up his hand. "Under both the sacred and the profane law, ignorance is no excuse for nonperformance of one's duties. Indeed, ignorance can be punished as an act of willful neglect, based upon the Total Personal Responsibility Act of '23, to say nothing of the Lesser Codicil." He smiled again. "However, there is no question of chastisement for you as yet."

"I'm glad to hear that, sir," Barrent said.

"'Uncle' is the proper form of address," the priest said. "I am Uncle Ingemar, and I have come to tell you about the orthodox religion of Omega, which is the worship of that pure and transcendent spirit of Evil which is our inspiration and our comfort."

Barrent said, "I'll be very happy to hear about the religion of Evil, Uncle. Shall we go into the living room?"

"By all means, Nephew," the priest said, and followed Barrent to the apartment in back of the store.

CHAPTER SIX

"Evil," the priest said, after he had settled comfortably into Barrent's best chair, "is that force within us which inspires men to acts of strength and endurance. The worship of Evil is essentially the worship of oneself, and therefore the only true worship. The self which one worships is the ideal social being; the man content in his niche in society, yet ready to grasp any opportunity for advancement; the man who meets death with dignity, who kills without the demeaning vice of pity. Evil is cruel, since it is a true reflection of the uncaring and insensate universe. Evil is eternal and unchanging, although it comes to us in the many forms of protean life."

"Would you care for a little wine, Uncle?" Barrent asked.

"Thank you, that's very thoughtful," Uncle Ingemar said. "How is business?"

"Fair. A little slow this week."

"People don't take the same interest in poisoning," the priest said, moodily sipping his drink. "Not like when I was a boy, newly unfrocked and shipped out from Earth. However. I was speaking to you about Evil."

"Yes, Uncle."

"We worship Evil," Uncle Ingemar said, "in the incarnate form of The Black One, that horned and horrid specter of our days and nights. In The Black One we find the seven cardinal sins, the forty felonies, and the hundred and one misdemeanors. There is no crime that The Black One has not performed—faultlessly, as befits his nature. Therefore we imperfect beings model ourselves upon his perfections. And sometimes, The Black One rewards us by appearing before us in the awful beauty of his fiery flesh. Yes, Nephew, I have actually been privileged to see him. Two years ago he appeared at the conclusion of the Games, and he also appeared the year before that."

The priest brooded for a moment over the divine appearance. Then he said, "Since we recognize in the State man's highest potential for Evil, we also worship the State as a suprahuman, though less than divine, creation."

Barrent nodded. He was having a difficult time staying awake. Uncle Ingemar's low, monotonous voice lecturing about so commonplace a thing as Evil had a soporific effect on him. He struggled to keep his eyes open.

"One might well ask," Uncle Ingemar droned on, "if Evil is the highest attainment of the nature of man, why then did The Black One allow any Good to exist in the universe? The problem of Good has bothered the unenlightened for ages. I will now answer it for you."

"Yes, Uncle?" Barrent said, surreptitiously pinching himself on the inside of the thigh in an effort to stay awake.

"But first," Uncle Ingemar said, "let us define our terms. Let us examine the nature of Good. Let us boldly and fearlessly stare our great opponent in the face and discover the true lineaments of his features."

"Yes," Barrent said, wondering if he should open a window. His eyes felt incredibly heavy. He rubbed them hard and tried to pay attention.

"Good is a state of illusion," said Uncle Ingemar in his even, monotonous voice, "which ascribes to man the nonexistent attributes of altruism, humility, and piety. How can we recognize Good as being an illusion? Because there is only man and The Black One in the universe, and to worship The Black One is to worship the ultimate expression of oneself. Thus, since we have proven Good to be an illusion, we necessarily recognize its attributes as nonexistent. Understood?"

Barrent didn't answer.

"Do you understand?" the priest asked more sharply.

"Eh?" Barrent said. He had been dozing with his eyes open. He forced himself awake and managed to say, "Yes, Uncle, I understand."

"Excellent. Understanding that, we ask, why did The Black One allow even the illusion of Good to exist in an Evil universe? And the answer is found in the Law of Necessary Opposites; for Evil could not be recognized as such without something to contrast it with. The best contrast is an opposite. And the opposite of Evil is Good." The priest smiled triumphantly. "It's so simple and clear-cut, isn't it?"

"It certainly is, Uncle," Barrent said. "Would you like a little more wine?"

"Just the tiniest drop," the priest said.

He talked to Barrent for another ten minutes about the natural and charming Evil inherent in the beasts of the field and forest, and counseled Barrent to pattern his behavior on those simple-minded creatures. At last he rose to leave.

"I'm very glad we could have this little chat," the priest said, warmly shaking Barrent's hand. "Can I count on your appearance at our Monday night services?"

"Services?"

"Of course," Uncle Ingemar said. "Every Monday night—at midnight—we hold Black Mass at the Wee Coven on Kirkwood Drive. After services, the Ladies Auxiliary usually puts out a snack, and we have community dancing and choir singing. It's all very jolly." He smiled broadly. "You see, the worship of evil *can* be fun."

"I'm sure it can," Barrent said. "I'll be there, Uncle."

He showed the priest to the door. After locking up, he thought carefully about what Uncle Ingemar had said. No doubt about it, attendance at services was necessary. Compulsory, in fact. He just hoped that the Black Mass wouldn't be as infernally dull as Ingemar's exposition of Evil.

That was Friday. Barrent was kept busy over the next two days. He received a shipment of homeopathic herbs and roots from his agent in the Bloodpit district. It took the better part of a day to sort and classify them, and another day to store them in the proper jars.

On Monday, returning to his shop after lunch, Barrent thought he saw the girl. He hurried after her, but lost her in the crowd.

When he got back to his store, Barrent found that a letter had been slipped under his door. It was an invitation from his neighborhood Dream Shop. The letter read:

> *Dear Citizen, We take this opportunity of welcoming you into the neighborhood and extending to you the services of what we believe to be the finest Dream on Omega.*
>
> *All manner and type of dreams are available to you—and at a surprisingly low cost. We specialize in memory-resurrecting dreams of Earth. You can be assured that your neighborhood Dream Shop offers you only the finest in vicarious living.*
>
> *As a Free Citizen, you will surely wish to avail yourself of these services. May we hope that you do so within the week?*
>
> *The Proprietors.*

Barrent put down the letter. He had no idea what a Dream Shop was, or how the dreams were produced. He would have to find out. Even though the invitation was graciously worded, it had a peremptory tone to it. Past a doubt, a visit to a Dream Shop was one of the obligations of a Free Citizen.

But of course, an obligation could be a pleasure, too. The Dream Shop sounded interesting. And a genuine memory-resurrection dream of Earth would be worth almost any price the proprietors wished to ask.

But that would have to wait. Tonight was Black Mass, and his attendance there was definitely required.

Barrent left his store at eleven o'clock in the evening. He wanted time for a stroll around Tetrahyde before going to the service, which began at midnight.

He started his walk with a definite sense of well-being. And yet, because of the irrational and unexpecting nature of Omega, he almost died before reaching the Wee Coven on Kirkwood Drive.

CHAPTER SEVEN

It had turned into a hot, almost suffocatingly humid night when Barrent began his walk. Not the faintest breath of air stirred along the darkened streets. Although he was wearing only a black mesh shirt, shorts, gunbelt, and sandals, Barrent felt as if he were wrapped in a thick blanket. Most of the people of Tetrahyde, except for those already at the Covens, had retired to the coolness of their cellars. The dark streets were nearly deserted.

Barrent walked on, more slowly. The few people he met were running to their homes. There was a sense of panic in that silent, dogged sprint through heat which made walking difficult. Barrent tried to find out what the matter was, but no one would stop. One old man shouted over his shoulder, "Get off the street, idiot!"

"Why?" Barrent asked him.

The old man snarled something unintelligible and hurried on.

Barrent kept on walking, nervously fingering the butt of his needlebeam. Something was certainly wrong, but he had no idea what it was. His nearest shelter now was the Wee Coven, about half a mile away. It seemed best to keep on moving in that direction, staying alert, waiting to see what was wrong.

In a few minutes, Barrent was alone in a tightly shuttered city. He moved into the center of the street, loosened the needlebeam in its holster, and prepared for attack from any side. Perhaps this was some special holiday like Landing Day.

Perhaps Free Citizens were fair game tonight. Anything seemed possible on a planet like Omega.

He thought he was ready for any possibility. But when the attack came, it was from an unexpected quarter.

A faint breeze stirred the stagnant air. It faded and returned, stronger this time, perceptibly cooling the hot streets. Wind rolled off the mountains of the interior and swept through the streets of Tetrahyde, and Barrent could feel the perspiration on his chest and back begin to dry.

For a few minutes, the climate of Tetrahyde was as pleasant as anything he could imagine.

Then the temperature continued to fall.

It dropped rapidly. Frigid air swept in from the distant mountain slopes, and the temperature fell through the seventies into the sixties.

This is ridiculous, Barrent thought to himself. I'd better get to the Coven.

He walked more rapidly, while the temperature plummeted. It passed through the forties into the low thirties. The first glittering signs of frost appeared on the streets.

It can't go much lower, Barrent thought.

But it could. An angry winter wind blew through the streets, and the temperature dropped into the twenties. Moisture in the air began forming into sleet.

Chilled to the bone, Barrent ran down the empty streets, and the wind, rising to gale force, pulled and tugged at him. The streets glittered with ice, making the footing dangerous. He skidded and fell, and had to run at a slower pace to keep his footing. And still the temperature dropped, and the wind growled and snapped like an angry beast.

He saw light through a heavily shuttered window. He stopped and pounded at the shutters, but no sound came from inside. He realized that the people of Tetrahyde never helped anyone; the more who died, the more chance there was for the survivors. So Barrent continued running, on feet that felt like chunks of wood.

The wind shrieked in his ear, and hailstones the size of his fist pelted the ground. He was getting too tired to run. All he could do now was walk, through a frozen white world, and hope he would reach the Wee Coven.

He walked for hours or for years. At one corner he passed the bodies of two men huddled against a wall and covered with frost. They had stopped running and had frozen to death.

Barrent forced himself to run again. A stitch in his side felt like a knife wound, and the cold was creeping up his arms and down his legs. Soon the cold would reach his chest, and that would be the end.

A flurry of hailstones stunned him. Without conscious transition he found that he was lying on the icy ground, and a monstrous wind was whirling away the tiny warmth his body was able to generate.

At the far end of the block he could see the tiny red light of the Coven. He crept toward it on hands and knees, moving mechanically, not really expecting to get there. He crawled forever, and the beckoning red light always remained the same distance from him.

But he kept on crawling, and at last he reached the door of the Coven. He pulled himself to his feet and turned the doorknob.

The door was locked.

He pounded feebly on the door. After a moment, a panel slid back. He saw a man staring at him; then the panel slid shut. He waited for the door to open. It didn't open. Minutes passed, and still it didn't open. What were they waiting for inside? What was wrong? Barrent tried to pound on the door again, lost his balance and fell to the ground. He rolled over and looked despairingly at the locked door. Then he lost consciousness.

WHEN HE came to, Barrent found himself lying on a couch. Two men were massaging his arms and legs, and beneath him he could feel the warmth of heating pads. Peering anxiously at him was the broad, swarthy face of Uncle Ingemar.

"Feeling better now?" Uncle Ingemar asked.

"I think so," Barrent said. "Why did you take so long opening the door?"

"We almost didn't open it at all," the priest told him. "It's against the law to aid strangers in distress. Since you hadn't as yet joined the Coven, you were technically still a stranger."

"Then why did you let me in?"

"My assistant noticed that we had an even number of worshipers. We require an odd number, preferably ending in three. Where the sacred and the profane laws are in conflict, the profane must yield. So we let you in despite the government ruling."

"It's a ridiculous ruling," Barrent said.

"Not really. Like most of the laws of Omega, it is designed to keep the population down. Omega is an extremely barren planet, you know. The constant arrival of new prisoners keeps swelling the population, to the enormous disadvantage of the older inhabitants. Ways and means must be sought to dispose of the excess newcomers."

"It isn't fair," Barrent said.

"You'll change your mind when you become an older inhabitant," Ingemar said. "And by your tenacity, I'm sure you'll become one."

"Maybe," Barrent said. "But what happened? The temperature must have dropped nearly a hundred degrees in fifteen minutes."

"A hundred and eight degrees to be exact," Uncle Ingemar said. "It's really very simple. Omega is a planet which revolves eccentrically around a double star system. Further instability, I'm told, comes from the planet's peculiar physical make-up— the placement of mountains and seas. The result is a uniformly and dramatically bad climate characterized by sudden violent temperature changes."

The assistant, a small, self-important fellow, said, "It has been calculated that Omega is at the outer limits of the planets which can support human life without gross artificial aids. If the fluctuations between hot and cold were any more violent, all human life here would be wiped out."

"It's the perfect punitive world," Uncle Ingemar said proudly. "Experienced residents sense when a temperature change is about to take place and get indoors."

"It's—hellish," Barrent said, at a loss for words.

"That describes it perfectly," the priest said. "It *is* hellish, and therefore perfect for the worship of The Black One. If you're feeling better now, Citizen Barrent, shall we proceed with services?"

Except for a touch of frostbite on his toes and fingers, Barrent was all right. He nodded, and followed the priest and the worshipers into the main part of the Coven.

After what he had been through, the Black Mass was necessarily an anticlimax. In his warmly heated pew, Barrent drowsed through Uncle Ingemar's sermon on the necessary performance of everyday evil.

The worship of Evil, Uncle Ingemar said, should not be reserved solely for Monday nights. On the contrary! The knowledge and performance of evil should suffuse one's daily life. It was not given to everyone to be a great sinner; but no one should be discouraged by that. Little acts of badness performed over a lifetime accumulated into a sinful whole most pleasing to The Black One. No one should forget that some of the greatest sinners, even the demoniac saints themselves, often had humble beginnings. Did not Thrastus start as a humble shopkeeper, cheating his customers of a portion of rice? Who would have expected that simple man to develop into the Red Slayer of Thorndyke Lane? And who could have imagined that Dr. Louen, son of a dockhand, would one day become the world's foremost authority on the practical applications of torture? Perseverance and piety had allowed those men to rise above their natural handicaps to a pre-eminent position at the right hand of The Black One. And it proved, Uncle Ingemar said, that Evil was the business of the poor as well as the rich.

That ended the sermon. Barrent awoke momentarily when the sacred symbols were brought out and displayed to the reverent congregation—a red-handled dagger, and a plaster toad. Then he dozed again through the slow inscribing of the magical pentagon.

At last the ceremony neared its end. The names of the interceding evil demons were read—Bael, Forcas, Buer, Marchocias, Astaroth, and Behemoth. A prayer was read to ward off the effects of Good. And Uncle Ingemar apologized for not having a virgin to sacrifice on the Red Altar.

"Our funds were not sufficient," he said, "for the purchase of a government-certified peon virgin. However, I am sure we will be able to perform the full ceremony next Monday. My assistant will now pass among you…"

The assistant carried around the black-rimmed collection plate. Like the other worshipers, Barrent contributed generously. It seemed wise to do so. Uncle Ingemar was clearly annoyed at not having a virgin to sacrifice. If he became a little angrier, he might take it into his head to sacrifice one of the congregation, virgin or not.

Barrent didn't stay for the choir singing or the community dancing. When the evening worship was finished, he poked his head cautiously out the door. The temperature had gone up to the seventies, and the frost was already melted from the ground. Barrent shook hands with the priest and hurried home.

CHAPTER EIGHT

Barrent had had enough of Omega's shocks and surprises. He stayed close to his store, worked at his business, and kept alert for trouble. He was beginning to develop the Omegan look: a narrow, suspicious squint, a hand always near gun butt, feet ready to sprint. Like the older inhabitants, he was acquiring a sixth sense for danger.

At night, after the doors and windows were barred and the triplex alarm system had been set, Barrent would lie on his bed and try to remember Earth. Probing into the misty recesses of his memory, he found tantalizing hints and traces, and fragments of pictures. Here was a great highway curving toward the sun; a fragment of a huge, multi-level city; a closeup view of a starship's curving hull. But the pictures were not continuous. They existed for the barest fraction of a second, then vanished.

On Saturday, Barrent spent the evening with Joe, Danis Foeren, and his neighbor Tem Rend. Joe's pokra had prospered, and he had been able to bribe his way to the status of Free Citizen. Foeren was too blunt and straightforward for that; he had remained at the Residency level. But Tem Rend promised to take the big forger as an assistant if the Assassin's Guild accepted his application.

The evening started pleasantly enough; but it ended, as usual, with an argument about Earth.

"Now look," Joe said, "we all know what Earth is like. It's a complex of gigantic floating cities. They're built on artificial islands in the various oceans—"

"No, the cities are on land," Barrent said.

"On water," Joe said. "The people of Earth have returned to the sea. Everyone has special oxygen adaptors for breathing salt water. The land areas aren't even used any more. The sea provides everything that—"

"It isn't like that," Barrent said. "I remember huge cities, but they were all on land."

Foeren said, "You're both wrong. What would Earth want with cities? She gave them up centuries ago. Earth is a landscaped park now. Everyone has his own home and several acres of land. All the forests and jungles have been allowed to grow back. People live *with* nature instead of trying to conquer it. Isn't that right, Tem?"

"Almost but not quite," Tem Rend said. "There are still cities, but they're underground. Tremendous underground factories and production areas. The rest is like Foeren said."

"There aren't any more factories," Foeren insisted stubbornly. "There's no need of them. Any goods which a man requires can be produced by thought-control."

"I'm telling you," Joe said, "I can remember the floating cities! I used to live in the Nimui sector on the island of Pasiphae."

"You think that proves anything?" Rend asked. "I remember that I worked on the eighteenth underground level of Nueva Chicaga. My work quota was twenty days a year. The rest of the time I spent outdoors in the forests—"

Foeren said, "That's wrong, Tem. There aren't any underground levels. I can remember distinctly that my father was a Controller, Third Class. Our family used to trek several hundred miles every year. When we needed something, my father would *think* it, and there it'd be. He promised to teach me how, but I guess he never did."

Barrent said, "Well, a couple of us are certainly having false recall."

"That's certain," Joe said. "But the question is, which of us is right?"

"We'll never find out," Rend said, "unless we can return to Earth."

That ended the discussion.

Toward the end of the week, Barrent received another invitation from the Dream Shop, more strongly worded than the first. He decided to discharge the obligation that evening. He checked the temperature, and found that it had risen into the high nineties. Wiser now in Omegan ways, he packed a small satchel full of cold-weather clothing, and started out.

The Dream Shop was located in the exclusive Death's Row section. Barrent went in, and found himself in a small, sumptuously furnished waiting room. A sleek young man behind a polished desk gave him an artificial smile.

"Could I be of service?" the young man asked. "My name is Nomis J. Arkdragen, assistant manager in charge of nightside dreams."

"I'd like to know something about what happens," Barrent said. "How one gets dreams, what kind of dreams, all that sort of thing."

"Of course," Arkdragen said. "Our service is easily explained, Citizen—"

"Barrent. Will Barrent."

Arkdragen nodded and checked a name from a list in front of him. He looked up and said, "Our dreams are produced by the action of drugs upon the brain and the central nervous system. There are many drugs which produce the desired effect. Among the most useful are heroin, morphine, opium, coca, hemp, and peyote. All those are Earth products. Found only on Omega are Black Slipper, nace, manicee, tri-narcotine, djedalas, and the various products of the carmoid group. Any and all of these are dream-inducers."

"I see," Barrent said. "Then you sell drugs."

"Not at all!" Arkdragen said. "Nothing so simple, nothing so crude. In ancient times on Earth, men administered drugs to themselves. The dreams which resulted were necessarily random in nature. You never knew what you would dream about, or for how long. You never knew if you would have a dream or a nightmare, a horror or a delight. This uncertainty has been removed from the modern Dream Shop. Nowadays, our drugs are carefully measured, mixed, and metered for each individual. There is an absolute precision in dream-making, ranging from the Nirvana-like calm of Black Slipper through the multicolored hallucinations of peyotl and tri-narcotine, to the sexual fantasies induced by nace and morphine, and at last to the memory-resurrecting dreams of the carmoid group."

"It's the memory-resurrecting dreams I'm interested in," Barrent said.

Arkdragen frowned. "I wouldn't recommend it for a first visit."

"Why not?"

"Dreams of Earth are apt to be more unsettling than any imaginary productions. It's usually advisable to build up a tolerance for them. I would advise a nice little sexual fantasy for your first visit. We have a special sale on sexual fantasies this week."

Barrent shook his head. "I think I'd prefer the real thing."

"You wouldn't," the assistant manager said, with a knowing smile. "Believe me, once one becomes accustomed to vicarious sex experiences, the real thing is pallid by comparison."

"Not interested," Barrent said. "What I want is a dream about Earth."

"But you haven't built up a tolerance!" Arkdragen said. "You aren't even addicted."

"Is addiction necessary?"

"It's important," Arkdragen told him, "as well as being inescapable. All our drugs are habit-forming, as the law requires. You see, to really appreciate a drug, you must build up a need for it. It heightens pleasure enormously, to say nothing of the increase in toleration. That's why I suggest that you begin with—"

"I want a dream about Earth," Barrent said.

"Very well," Arkdragen said grudgingly. "But we will not be responsible for any traumas which accrue."

He led Barrent into a long passageway. It was lined with doors, and behind some of them Barrent could hear dull moans and gasps of pleasure.

"Experiencers," Arkdragen said, without further explanation. He took Barrent to an open room near the end of the corridor. Within sat a cheerful-looking bearded man in a white coat reading a book.

"Good evening, Doctor Wayn," Arkdragen said. "This is Citizen Barrent. First visit. He insists upon an Earth dream." Arkdragen turned and left.

"Well," the doctor said, "I guess we can manage that." He put down his book. "Just lie down over there, Citizen Barrent."

In the center of the room was a long, adjustable table. Above it hung a complicated-looking instrument. At the end of the room were glass-sided cabinets filled with square jars; they reminded Barrent of his antidotes.

He lay down. Doctor Wayn put him through a general examination, then a specific check for suggestibility, hypnotic index, reactions to the eleven basic drug groups, and susceptibility to tetanic and epileptic seizures. He jotted down his results on a pad, checked his figures, went to a cabinet, and began mixing drugs.

"Is this likely to be dangerous?" Barrent asked.

"It shouldn't be," Doctor Wayn said. "You appear healthy enough. Quite healthy, in fact, and with a low suggestibility rating. Of course, epileptic fits *do* occur, probably because of cumulative allergic reactions. Can't help that sort of thing. And then there are the traumas, which sometimes result in insanity and death. They form an interesting study in themselves. And some people get stuck in their dreams and are unable to be extricated. I suppose that could be classified as a form of insanity, although actually it isn't."

The doctor had finished mixing his drugs. He was loading a hypodermic with the mixture. Barrent was having serious doubts about the advisability of the whole thing.

"Perhaps I should postpone this visit," he said. "I'm not sure that I—"

"Don't worry about a thing," the doctor said. "This is the finest Dream Shop on Omega. Try to relax. Tight muscles can result in tetanic convulsions."

"I think Mr. Arkdragen was right," Barrent said. "Maybe I shouldn't have a dream about Earth for my first visit. He said it was dangerous."

"Well, after all," the doctor said, "what's life without a little risk? Besides, the most common damage is brain lesions and burst blood vessels. And we have full facilities for taking care of that sort of thing."

He poised the hypodermic over Barrent's left arm.

"I've changed my mind," Barrent said, and started to get off the bed. Doctor Wayn deftly slid the needle into Barrent's arm.

"One does not change one's mind," he told Barrent, "inside a Dream Shop. Try to relax…"

Barrent relaxed. He lay back on the bed, and heard a shrill singing in his ears. He tried to focus on the doctor's face. But the face had changed.

The face was old, round, and fleshy. Ridges of fat stood out on the chin and neck. The face was perspiring, friendly, worried.

It was Barrent's 5th Term Advisor.

"Now, Will," the Advisor said, "you must be careful. You must learn to restrain that temper of yours. Will, you *must*!"

"I know, sir," Barrent said. "It's just that I get so mad at that—"

"Will!"

"All right," Barrent said. "I'll watch myself."

He left the university office and walked into the city. It was a fantastic city of skyscrapers and multi-level streets, a brilliant city of silver and diamond hues, an ambitious city which administered a far-flung network of countries and planets. Barrent walked along the third pedestrian level, still angry, thinking about Andrew Therkaler.

Because of Therkaler and his ridiculous jealousy, Barrent's application for the Space Exploration Corps had been turned down. There was nothing his Advisor could do about the matter; Therkaler had too much influence on the Selection Board. It would be a full three years before Barrent could apply again. In the meantime he was Earth-bound and unemployable. All his studies had been for extraterrestrial exploration. There was no place for him on Earth; and now he was barred from space.

Therkaler!

Barrent left the pedestrian level and took the highspeed ramp into the Sante district. As the ramp moved, he fingered the small weapon in his pocket. Handguns were illegal on Earth. He had procured his through untraceable means.

He was determined to kill Therkaler.

There was a wash of grotesque faces. The dream blurred. When it cleared, Barrent found himself aiming his handgun at a thin, cross-eyed fellow whose scream for mercy was abruptly cut short.

The informer, blank-faced and stern, noted the crime and informed the police.

The police, in uniforms of gray, took him into custody and brought him before the judge.

The judge, with his vague parchment face, sentenced him to perpetual servitude upon the planet Omega, and handed down the obligatory decree that Barrent be cleansed of memory.

Then the dream turned into a kaleidoscope of horror. Barrent was climbing a slippery pole, a sheer mountainside, a smooth-sided well. Behind him, gaining on him, was Therkaler's corpse with its chest ripped open. Supporting the corpse on either side were the blank-faced informer and the parchment-faced judge.

Barrent ran down a hill, a street, a rooftop. His pursuers were close behind him. He entered a dim yellow room, closed and locked the door. When he turned around, he saw that he had locked himself in with Therkaler's corpse. Fungus was blossoming in the open wound in the chest, and the scarred head was crowned with red and purple mold. The corpse advanced, reached for him, and Barrent dived headfirst through the window.

"Come out of it, Barrent. You're overdoing it. Come out of the dream."

Barrent had no time to listen. The window turned into a chute, and he slid down its polished sides into an amphitheatre. There, across gray sand, the corpse crept toward him on the stubs of arms and legs. The enormous grandstand was empty except for the judge and the informer, who sat side by side, watching.

"He's stuck."

"Well, I warned him…"

"Come out of the dream, Barrent. This is Doctor Wayn. You're on Omega, in the Dream Shop. Come out of the dream. There's still time if you pull yourself out immediately."

Omega? Dream? There was no time to think about it. Barrent was swimming across a dark, evil-smelling lake. The judge and the informer were swimming just behind him, flanking the corpse, whose skin was slowly peeling away.

"Barrent!"

And now the lake was turning into a thick jelly which clung to his arms and legs and filled his mouth, while the judge and the informer—

"Barrent!"

Barrent opened his eyes and found himself on the adjustable bed in the Dream Shop. Doctor Wayn, looking somewhat shaken, was standing over him. A nurse was near by with a tray of hypodermics and an oxygen mask. Behind her was Arkdragen, wiping perspiration from his forehead.

"I didn't think you were going to make it," Doctor Wayn said. "I really didn't."

"He pulled out just in time," the nurse said.

"I warned him," Arkdragen said, and left the room.

Barrent sat up. "What happened?" he asked.

Doctor Wayn shrugged his shoulders. "It's hard to tell. Perhaps you were prone to circular reaction; and sometimes the drugs aren't absolutely pure. But these things usually don't happen more than once. Believe me, Citizen Barrent, the drug experience is very pleasant. I'm sure you'll enjoy it the second time."

Still shaken by his experience, Barrent was certain there would be no second time for him. Whatever the cost, he was not going to risk a repetition of that nightmare.

"Am I addicted now?" he asked.

"Oh, no," Doctor Wayn said. "Addiction occurs with the third or fourth visit."

Barrent thanked him and left. He passed Arkdragen's desk and asked how much he owed.

"Nothing," Arkdragen said. "The first visit is always on the house." He gave Barrent a knowing smile.

Barrent left the Dream Shop and hurried home to his apartment. He had a lot to think about. Now, for the first time, he had proof that he was a willful and premeditated murderer.

CHAPTER NINE

Being accused of a murder you can't remember is one thing; remembering a murder you have been accused of is another thing entirely. Such evidence is hard to disbelieve.

Barrent tried to sort out his feelings on the matter. Before his visit to the Dream Shop he had never felt himself a murderer, no matter what the Earth authorities had accused him of. At worst, he had thought that he might have killed a man in a sudden uncontrollable fit of rage. But to plan and perform a murder in cold blood...

Why had he done it? Had his lust for revenge been so great as to throw off all the restraint of Earth's civilization? Apparently so. He had killed, and someone had informed on him, and a judge had sentenced him to Omega. He was a murderer on a criminal's planet. To live here successfully, he simply had to follow his natural bias toward murder.

And yet, Barrent found this extremely difficult to do. He had surprisingly little taste for bloodshed. On Free Citizen's Day, although he went into the streets with his needlebeam, he couldn't bring himself to slaughter any of the lower classes. He didn't want to kill. It was a ridiculous prejudice, considering where and what he was; but there it was. No matter how often Tem Rend or Joe lectured him on his Citizen's duties, Barrent still found murder quite distasteful.

He sought the aid of a psychiatrist, who told him that his rejection of murder had its roots in an unhappy childhood. The phobia had been further complicated by the traumatic qualities of his experience in the Dream Shop. Because of this, murder, the highest social good, had become repugnant to him. This antimurder neurosis in a man eminently suited for the art of killing would, the psychiatrist said, inevitably lead to Barrent's destruction. The only solution was to displace the neurosis. The psychiatrist suggested immediate treatment in a sanitarium for the criminally non-murderous.

Barrent visited a sanitarium, and heard the mad inmates screaming about goodness, fair play, the sanctity of life, and other obscenities. He had no intention of joining them. Perhaps he was sick, but he wasn't *that* sick!

His friends told him that his uncooperative attitude was bound to get him into trouble. Barrent agreed; but he hoped, by killing only when it became necessary, that he would escape the observation of the highly placed individuals who administered the law.

For several weeks his plan seemed to work. He ignored the increasingly peremptory notes from the Dream Shop and did not return to services at the Wee Coven. Business prospered, and Barrent spent his spare time studying the effects of the rarer poisons and practicing with his needlebeam. He often thought about the girl. He still had the gun she had lent him. He wondered if he would ever see her again.

And he thought about Earth. Since his visit to the Dream Shop, he had occasional flashes of recall, isolated pictures of a weathered stone building, a stand of live oaks, the curve of a river seen through willows. This half-remembered Earth filled him with an almost unbearable longing. Like most of the citizens of Omega, his only real wish was to go home.

And that was impossible.

The days passed, and when trouble came, it came unexpectedly. One night there was a heavy knocking at his door. Half asleep, Barrent answered it. Four uniformed men pushed their way inside and told him he was under arrest.

"What for?" Barrent asked.

"Non-drug addiction," one of the men told him. "You have three minutes to dress."

"What's the penalty?"

"You'll find out in court," the man said. He winked at the other guards and added, "But the only way to cure a nonaddict is to kill him. Eh?"

Barrent dressed.

HE WAS taken to a room in the sprawling Department of Justice. The room was called the Kangaroo Court, in honor of ancient Anglo-Saxon judicial proceeding. Across the hall from it, also of antique derivation, was the Star Chamber. Just past that was the Court of Last Appeal.

The Kangaroo Court was divided in half by a high wooden screen, for it was fundamental to Omegan justice that the accused should not see his judge nor any of the witnesses against him.

"Let the prisoner rise," a voice said from behind the screen. The voice, thin, flat and emotionless, came through a small amplifier. Barrent could barely understand the words; tone and inflection were lost, as had been planned for. Even in speaking, the judge remained anonymous.

"Will Barrent," the judge said, "you have been brought before this court on a major charge of non-drug addiction and a minor charge of religious impiety. On the minor count we have the sworn statement of a priest. On the major count we have the testimony of the Dream Shop. Can you refute either of these charges?"

Barrent thought for a moment, then answered, "No, sir, I can't."

"For the present," the judge said, "your religious impiety can be waived, since it is a first offense. But non-drug addiction is a major crime against the state of Omega. The uninterrupted use of drugs is an enforced privilege of every citizen. It is well known that privileges must be exercised, otherwise they will be lost. To lose our privileges would be to lose the very cornerstone of our liberty. Therefore to reject or otherwise fail to perform a privilege is tantamount to high treason."

There was a pause. The guards shuffled their feet restlessly. Barrent, who considered his situation hopeless, stood at attention and waited.

"Drugs serve many purposes," the hidden judge went on. "I need not enumerate their desirable qualities for the user. But speaking from the viewpoint of the state, I will tell you that an addicted populace is a loyal populace; that drugs are a major source of tax revenue; that drugs exemplify our entire way of life. Furthermore, I say to you that the nonaddicted minorities have invariably proven hostile to native Omegan institutions. I give you this lengthy explanation, Will Barrent, in order that you may better understand the sentence which is to be passed upon you."

"Sir," Barrent said, "I was wrong in avoiding addiction. I won't plead ignorance, because I know the law doesn't recognize that excuse. But I will ask you most humbly for another chance. I ask you to remember, sir, that addiction and rehabilitation are still possible for me."

"The court recognizes that," the judge said. "For that reason, the court is pleased to exercise its fullest powers of judicial mercy. Instead of summary execution, you may choose between two lesser decrees. The first is punitive; that you shall suffer the loss of your right hand and left leg in atonement for your crime against the State; but that you shall not lose your life."

Barrent gulped and asked, "What is the other decree, sir?"

"The other decree, which is nonpunitive, is that you shall undergo a Trial by Ordeal. And that, if you survive such a trial, you shall be returned to appropriate rank and position in society."

"I'll take the Trial by Ordeal," Barrent said.

"Very well," said the judge. "Let the case proceed."

Barrent was led from the room. Behind him, he heard a quickly concealed laugh from one of the guards. Had he chosen wrong? he wondered. Could a trial by ordeal be worse than outright mutilation?

CHAPTER TEN

On Omega, so the saying went, you couldn't fit a knife blade between the trial and the execution of the sentence. Barrent was taken at once to a large, circular stone room in the basement of the Department of Justice. White arc lights glared down at him from a high, arched ceiling. Below, one section of wall had been cut away to provide a reviewing stand for spectators. The stands were almost filled when Barrent arrived, and hawkers were selling copies of the day's legal calendar.

For a few moments Barrent was alone on the stone floor. Then a panel slid away in one curved wall, and a small machine rolled out.

A loudspeaker set high in the reviewing stand announced, "Ladies and gentlemen, your attention please! You are about to witness Trial 642-BG223, by Ordeal, between Citizen Will Barrent and GME 213. Take your seats, please. The contest will begin in a few minutes."

Barrent looked over his opponent. It was a glistening black machine shaped like a half-sphere, standing almost four feet high. It rolled restlessly back and forth on small wheels. A pattern of red, green, and amber lights from recessed glass bulbs flashed across its smooth metal hide. It stirred in Barrent a vague memory of some creature from Earth's oceans.

"For the benefit of those who are visiting our gallery for the first time," the loudspeaker said, "a word of explanation is in order. The prisoner, Will Barrent, has freely chosen the Trial by Ordeal. The instrument of justice, which in this instance is GME 213, is an example of the finest creative engineering which Omega has produced. The machine, or Max, as its many friends and admirers call it, is a murder weapon of exemplary efficiency, able to utilize no less than twenty-three killing modes, many of them extremely painful. For trial purposes, it is set to operate upon a random principle. This means that Max has no choice over the way in which it kills. The modes are selected and abandoned by a random arrangement of twenty-three numbers, linked to an equally random time-selection of one to six seconds."

Max suddenly moved toward the center of the room, and Barrent backed away from it.

"It is within the prisoner's power," the loudspeaker voice continued, "to disable the machine; in which case, the prisoner wins the contest and is set free with full rights and privileges of his station. The method of disabling varies from machine to machine. It is always theoretically possible for a prisoner to win. Practically speaking, this has happened on an average of 3.5 times out of a hundred."

Barrent looked up at the gallery of spectators. To judge by their dress, they were all men and women of status; high in the ranks of the Privileged Classes.

Then he saw, sitting in a front row seat, the girl who had lent him her gun on his first day in Tetrahyde. She was as beautiful as he had remembered her; but no hint of emotion touched her pale, oval face. She stared at him with the frank and detached interest of someone watching an unusual bug under a jar.

"Let the contest begin!" the loudspeaker announced.

Barrent had no more time to think about the girl, for the machine was rolling toward him.

He circled warily away from it. Max extruded a single slender tentacle with a white light winking in the end of it The machine rolled toward Barrent, backing him toward a wall.

Abruptly it stopped. Barrent heard the clank of gears. The tentacle was withdrawn, and in its place appeared a jointed metal arm which ended in a knife-edge. Moving more quickly now, the machine cornered him against the wall. The arm flickered out, but Barrent managed to dodge it. He heard the knife-edge scrape against stone. When the arm withdrew, Barrent had a chance to move again into the center of the room.

He knew that his only chance to disable the machine was during the pause when its selector changed it from one killing mode to another. But how do you disable a smooth-surfaced turtle-backed machine?

Max came at him again, and now its metal hide glistened with a dull green substance which Barrent immediately recognized as Contact Poison. He broke into a spring, circling the room, trying to avoid the fatal touch.

The machine stopped. Neutralizer washed over its surface, clearing away the poison. Then the machine was coming toward him again, this time with no weapons visible, apparently intending to ram.

Barrent was badly winded. He dodged, and the machine dodged with him. He was standing against the wall, helpless, as the machine picked up speed.

It stopped, inches from him. Its selector clicked. Max was extruding some sort of a club.

This, Barrent thought, was an exercise in applied sadism. If it went on much longer, the machine would run him off his feet and kill him at its leisure. Whatever he was going to do, he had better do it at once, while he still had the strength.

Even as he thought that, the machine swung a clubbed metal arm. Barrent couldn't avoid the blow completely. The club struck his left shoulder, and he felt his arm go numb.

Max was selecting again. Barrent threw himself on its smooth, rounded back. At the very top he saw two tiny holes. Praying that they were air intake openings, Barrent plugged them with his fingers.

The machine stopped dead, and the audience roared. Barrent clung to the smooth surface with his numbed arm, trying to keep his fingers in the holes. The pattern of lights on Max's surface changed from green through amber to red. Its deep-throated buzz became a dull hum.

And then the machine extruded tubes as alternative intake holes.

Barrent tried to cover them with his body. But the machine, roaring into sudden life, swiveled rapidly and threw him off.

Barrent rolled to his feet and moved back to the center of the arena.

The contest had lasted no more than five minutes, but Barrent was exhausted. He forced himself to retreat from the machine, which was coming at him now with a broad, gleaming hatchet.

As the hatchet-arm swung, Barrent threw himself *at* it instead of away. He caught the arm in both hands and bent it back. Metal creaked, and Barrent thought he could hear the joint beginning to give way. If he could break off the metal arm, he might disable the machine; at the very least, the arm would be a weapon...

Max suddenly went into reverse. Barrent tried to keep his grip on the arm, but it was yanked away. He fell on his face. The hatchet swung, gouging his shoulder.

Barrent rolled over and looked at the gallery. He was finished. He might as well accept the machine's next attempt gracefully and have it over with. The spectators were cheering, watching Max begin its transformation into another killing mode.

And the girl was motioning to him.

Barrent stared, trying to make some sense out of it. She gestured at him to turn something over, turn it over and destroy.

He had no more time to watch. Dizzy from loss of blood, he staggered to his feet and watched the machine charge. He didn't bother to see what weapon it had extruded; his entire attention was concentrated on its wheels.

As it came at him, Barrent threw himself under the wheels.

The machine tried to brake and swerve, but not in time. The wheels rolled onto Barrent's body, tilting the machine sharply upward. Barrent grunted under the impact. With his back under the machine, he put his remaining strength in an attempt to stand up.

For a moment the machine teetered, its wheels spinning wildly. Then it flipped over on its back. Barrent collapsed beside it.

When he could see again, the machine was still on its back. It was extruding a set of arms to turn itself over.

Barrent threw himself on the machine's flat belly and hammered with his fists. Nothing happened. He tried to pull off one of the wheels, and couldn't. Max was propping itself up, preparing to turn over and resume the contest.

The girl's motions caught Barrent's eye. She was making a plucking motion, repeatedly, insistently.

Only then Barrent saw a small fuse box near one of the wheels. He yanked off the cover, losing most of a fingernail in the process, and removed the fuse.

The machine expired gracefully.

Barrent fainted.

CHAPTER ELEVEN

On Omega, the law is supreme. Hidden and revealed, sacred and profane, the law governs the actions of all citizens, from the lowest of the low to the highest of the high. Without the law, there could be no privileges for those who made the law; therefore the law was absolutely necessary. Without the law and its stern enforcement, Omega would be an unthinkable chaos in which a man's rights could extend only as far and as long as he personally could enforce them. This anarchy would mean the end of Omegan society; and particularly, it would mean the end of those senior citizens of the ruling class who had grown high in status, but whose skill with a gun had long passed its peak.

Therefore the law was necessary.

But Omega was also a criminal society, composed entirely of individuals who had broken the laws of Earth. It was a society which, in the final analysis, stressed individual endeavor. It was a society in which the lawbreaker was king; a society in which crimes were not only condoned but were admired and even rewarded; a society in which deviation from the rules was judged solely on its degree of success.

And this resulted in the paradox of a criminal society with absolute laws which were meant to be broken.

The judge, still hidden behind his screen, explained all this to Barrent. Several hours had passed since the end of the Trial by Ordeal. Barrent had been taken to the infirmary, where his injuries were patched up. They were minor, for the most part; two cracked ribs, a deep gouge in his left shoulder, and various cuts and bruises.

"Accordingly," the judge went on, "the law must simultaneously be broken and not broken. Those who never break a law never rise in status. They are usually killed off in one way or another, since they lack the necessary initiative to survive. For those who, like yourself, break laws, the situation is somewhat different. The law punishes them with absolute severity—*unless they can get away with it.*"

The judge paused. In a thoughtful voice he continued, "The highest type of man on Omega is the individual who understands the laws, appreciates their necessity, knows the penalties for infraction, then breaks them—and succeeds! That, sir, is your ideal criminal and your ideal Omegan. And that is what you have succeeded in doing, Will Barrent, by winning the Trial by Ordeal."

"Thank you, sir," Barrent said.

"I wish you to understand," the judge continued, "that success in breaking the law once does not imply that you will succeed a second time. The odds are increasingly against you each time you try—just as the rewards are increasingly greater if you succeed. Therefore I counsel you not to act rashly upon your new acquisition of knowledge."

"I won't, sir," Barrent said.

"Very well. You are hereby elevated to the status of Privileged Citizen, with all the rights and obligations which that entails. You are allowed to keep your business, as before. Furthermore, you are granted a week's free vacation in the Lake of Clouds region; and you may go on that vacation with any female of your choice."

"I beg pardon?" Barrent said. "What was that last?"

"A week's vacation," the hidden judge repeated, "with any female of your choice. It is a high reward, since men outnumber women on Omega by six to one. You may pick any unmarried woman, willing or unwilling. I will grant you three days in which to make a choice."

"I don't need three days," Barrent said. "I want the girl who was sitting in the front row of the spectators' gallery. The girl with black hair and green eyes. Do you know which one I mean?"

"Yes," the judge said slowly, "I know which one you mean. Her name is Moera Ermais. I suggest that you choose someone else."

"Is there any reason?"

"No. But you would be much better advised if you selected someone else. My clerk will be pleased to furnish you with a list of suitable young ladies. All of them have affidavits of good performance. Several are graduates of the Women's Institute, which, as you perhaps know, gives a rigorous two-year course in the geishan arts and sciences. I can personally recommend your attention to—"

"Moera is the one I want," Barrent said.

"Young man, you err in your judgment."

"I'll have to take that chance."

"Very well," the judge said. "Your vacation starts at nine tomorrow morning. I sincerely wish you good fortune."

GUARDS ESCORTED Barrent from the judge's chambers, and he was taken back to his shop. His friends, who had been waiting for the death announcement, came to congratulate him. They were eager to hear the complete details of the Trial by Ordeal; but Barrent had learned now that secret knowledge was the road to power. He gave them only the sketchiest outline.

There was another cause for celebration that night. Tem Rend's application had finally been accepted by the Assassin's

Guild. As he had promised, he was taking Foeren on as his assistant.

The following morning, Barrent opened his shop and saw a vehicle in front of his door. It had been provided for his vacation by the Department of Justice. Sitting in the back, looking beautiful and very annoyed, was Moera.

She said, "Are you out of your mind, Barrent? Do you think I have time for this sort of thing? Why did you pick me?"

"You saved my life," Barrent said.

"And I suppose you think that means I'm interested in you? Well, I'm not. If you have any gratitude, you'll tell the driver that you've changed your mind. You can still choose another girl."

Barrent shook his head. "You're the only girl I'm interested in."

"Then you won't reconsider?"

"Not a chance."

Moera sighed and leaned back. "Are you *really* interested in me?"

"Much more than interested," Barrent said.

"Well," Moera said, "if you won't change your mind, I suppose I'll just have to put up with you." She turned away; but before she did, Barrent caught the faintest suggestion of a smile.

CHAPTER TWELVE

The Lake of Clouds was Omega's finest vacation resort. Upon entering the district, all weapons had to be checked at the main gate. No duels were allowed under any circumstances. Quarrels were arbitrarily decided by the nearest barman, and murder was punished by immediate loss of all status.

Every amusement was available at the Lake of Clouds. There were the exhibitions such as fencing bouts, bull fighting, and bear baiting. There were sports like swimming, mountain climbing, and skiing. In the evenings there was dancing in the main ballroom, behind glass walls which separated residents from citizens and citizens from the elite. There was a well-stocked drug bar containing anything the fashionable addict could desire, as well as a few novelties he might wish to sample. For the gregarious, there was an orgy every Wednesday and Saturday night in the Satyr's Grotto. For the shy, the management arranged masked trysts in the dim passageways beneath the hotel. But most important of all, there were gently rolling hills and shadowy woods to walk in, free from the tensions of the daily struggle for existence in Tetrahyde.

Barrent and Moera had adjoining rooms, and the door between them was unlocked. But on the first night, Barrent did not go through the door. Moera had given no sign of wanting him to do so; and on a planet where women have easy and continual access to poisons, a man had to think twice before inflicting his company where it was not wanted. Even the owner of an antidote shop had to consider the possibility of not being able to recognize his own symptoms in time.

On their second day, they climbed high into the hills. They ate a basket lunch on a grassy incline which sloped away to the gray sea. After they had eaten, Barrent asked Moera why she had saved his life.

"You won't like the answer," she told him.

"I'd still like to hear it."

"Well, you looked so ridiculously vulnerable that day in the Victim's Society. I would have helped anyone who looked that way."

Barrent nodded uncomfortably. "What about the second time?"

"By then I suppose I had an interest in you. Not a romantic interest, you understand. I'm not at all romantic."

"What kind of an interest?" Barrent asked.

"I thought you might be good recruitment material."

"I'd like to hear more about it," Barrent said.

Moera was silent for a while, watching him with unblinking green eyes. She said, "There's not much I can tell you. I'm a member of an organization. We're always on the lookout for good prospects. Usually we screen directly from the prison ships. After that, recruiters like me go out in search of people we can use."

"What type of people do you look for?"

"Not your type, Will. I'm sorry."

"Why not me?"

"At first I thought seriously about recruiting you," Moèra said. "You seemed like just the sort of person we needed. Then I checked into your record."

"And?"

"We don't recruit murderers. Sometimes we employ them for specific jobs, but we don't take them into the organization. There are certain extenuating circumstances which we recognize; self-defense, for example. But aside from that, we feel that a man who has committed premeditated murder on Earth is the wrong man for us."

"I see," Barrent said. "Would it help any if I told you I don't have the usual Omegan attitude toward murder?"

"I know you don't," Moera said. "If it were up to me, I'd take you into the organization. But it's not my choice... Will, are you sure you're a murderer?"

"I believe I am," Barrent said. "I probably am."

"Too bad," Moera said. "Still, the organization needs high-survival types, no matter what they did on Earth. I can't promise anything, but I'll see what I can do. It would help if you could find out more about why you committed murder. Perhaps there were extenuating circumstances."

"Perhaps," Barrent said doubtfully. "I'll try to find out."

That evening, just before he went to sleep, Moera opened the adjoining door and came into his room. Slim and warm, she slipped into his bed. When he started to speak, she put a hand over his mouth. And Barrent, who had learned not to question good fortune, kept quiet.

The rest of the vacation passed much too quickly. The subject of the organization did not come up again; but, perhaps as compensation, the adjoining door was not closed. At last, late on the seventh day, Barrent and Moera returned to Tetrahyde.

"When can I see you again?" Barrent asked.

"I'll get in touch with you."

"That's not a very satisfactory arrangement."

"It's the best I can do," Moera said. "I'm sorry, Will. I'll see what I can do about the organization."

Barrent had to be satisfied with that. When the vehicle dropped him at his store, he still didn't know where she lived, or what kind of an organization she represented.

BACK IN his apartment, he considered carefully the details of his dream in the Dream Shop. It was all there: his anger at Therkaler, the illicit weapon, the encounter, the corpse, and then the informer and the judge. Only one thing was missing. He had no recollection of the actual murder, no memory of aiming the weapon and activating it. The dream stopped when he met Therkaler, and started again after he was dead.

Perhaps he had blocked the moment of actual murder out of his mind; but perhaps there had been some provocation, some satisfactory reason why he had killed the man. He would have to find out.

There were only two ways of getting information about Earth. One lay through the horror-tinged visions of the Dream Shop, and he was determined not to go there again. The other way was through the services of a skrenning mutant.

Barrent had the usual distaste for mutants. They were another race entirely, and their status of untouchability was no mere prejudice. It was well known that mutants often carried strange and incurable diseases. They were shunned, and they had reacted to exclusion by exclusiveness. They lived in the Mutant Quarter, which was almost a self-contained city within Tetrahyde. Citizens with good sense stayed away from the Quarter, especially after dark; everyone knew that mutants could be vindictive.

But only mutants had the skrenning ability. In their misshapen bodies were unusual powers and talents, odd and abnormal abilities which the normal man shunned by day but secretly courted by night. Mutants were said to be in the particular favor of The Black One. Some people felt that the great art of Black Magic, about which the priests boasted, could only be performed by a mutant; but one never said so in the presence of a priest.

Mutants, because of their strange talents, were reputed to remember much more of Earth than was possible for normal men and women. Not only could they remember Earth in general, but in particular they could skren the life-thread of a man backward through space and time, pierce the wall of forgetfulness and tell what really had happened to him.

Other people believed that mutants had no unusual abilities at all. They considered them clever rogues who lived off people's credulity.

Barrent decided to find out for himself. Late one night, suitably cloaked and armed, he left his apartment and went to the Mutant Quarter.

CHAPTER THIRTEEN

Barrent walked through the narrow, twisting streets of the Quarter, one hand never far from his weapon. He walked among the lame and the blind, past hydrocephaloid and microcephalous idiots, past a juggler who kept twelve flaming torches in the air with the aid of a rudimentary third hand growing out of his chest. There were vendors selling clothing, charms, and jewelry. There were carts loaded with pungent and unsanitary-looking food. He walked past a row of brightly painted brothels. Girls crowded the windows and shrieked at him, and a four-armed, six-legged woman told him he was just in time for the Delphian Rites. Barrent turned away from her and almost ran into a monstrously fat woman who pulled open her blouse to reveal eight shrunken breasts. He ducked around her, moving quickly past four linked Siamese quadruplets who stared at him with huge mournful eyes.

Barrent turned a corner and stopped. A tall, ragged old man with a cane was blocking his way. The man was half-blind; the skin had grown smooth and hairless over the socket where his left eye should have been. But his right eye was sharp and fierce under a white eyebrow.

"You wish the services of a genuine skrenner?" the old man asked.

Barrent nodded.

"Follow me," the mutant said. He turned into an alley, and Barrent came after him, gripping the butt of his needlebeam tightly. Mutants were forbidden by law to carry arms; but like this old man, most of them had heavy, iron-headed walking sticks. At close quarters, no one could ask for a better weapon.

The old man opened a door and motioned Barrent inside. Barrent paused, thinking about the stories he had heard of gullible citizens falling into mutant hands. Then he half-drew his needlebeam and went inside.

At the end of a long passageway, the old man opened a door and led Barrent into a small, dimly lighted room. As his eyes became accustomed to the dark, Barrent could make out the shapes of two women sitting in front of a plain wooden table. There was a pan of water on the table, and in the pan was a fist-sized piece of glass cut into many facets.

One of the women was very old and completely hairless. The other was young and beautiful. As Barrent moved closer to the table, he saw, with a sense of shock, that her legs were joined below the knee by a membrane of scaly skin, and her feet were of a rudimentary fish-tail shape.

"What do you wish us to skren for you, Citizen Barrent?" the young woman asked.

"How did you know my name?" Barrent asked. When he got no answer, he said, "All right. I want to find out about a murder I committed on Earth."

"Why do you want to find out about it?" the young woman asked. "Won't the authorities credit it to your record?"

"They credit it. But I want to find out why I did it. Maybe there were extenuating circumstances. Maybe I did it in self-defense."

"Is it really important?" the young woman asked.

"I think so," Barrent said. He hesitated a moment, then took the plunge. "The fact of the matter is, I have a neurotic prejudice against murder. I would rather *not* kill. So I want to find out why I committed murder on Earth."

The mutants looked at each other. Then the old man grinned and said, "Citizen, we'll help you all we can. We mutants also have a prejudice against killing, since it's always someone else killing us. We're all in favor of citizens with a neurosis against murder."

"Then you'll skren my past?"

"It's not as easy as that," the young woman said. "The skrenning ability, which is one of a cluster of psi talents, is difficult to use. It doesn't always function. And when it does function, it often doesn't reveal what it's supposed to."

"I thought all mutants could look into the past whenever they wanted to," Barrent said.

"No," the old man told him, "that isn't true. For one thing, not all of us who are classified mutants are true mutants. Almost any deformity or abnormality these days is called mutantism. It's a handy term to cover anyone who doesn't conform to the Terran standard of appearance."

"But some of you are true mutants?"

"Certainly. But even then, there are different types of mutantism. Some just show radiation abnormalities—giantism, microcephaly, and the like. Only a few of us possess the slightest psi abilities—although all mutants claim them."

"Are you able to skren?" Barrent asked him.

"No. But Myla can," he said, pointing to the young woman. "Sometimes she can."

The young woman was staring into the pan of water, into the faceted glass. Her pale eyes were open very wide, showing almost all pupil, and her fish-tailed body was rigidly upright, supported by the old woman.

"She's beginning to see something," the man said. "The water and the glass are just devices to focus her attention. Myla's good at skrenning, though sometimes she gets the future confused with the past. That sort of thing is embarrassing, and it gives skrenning a bad name. It can't be helped, though. Every once in a while the future is there in the water, and Myla has to tell what she sees. Last week she told a Hadji he was going to die in four days." The old man chuckled. "You should have seen the expression on his face."

"Did she see how he would die?" Barrent asked.

"Yes. By a knife-thrust. The poor man stayed in his house for the entire four days."

"Was he killed?"

"Of course. His wife killed him. She was a strong-minded woman, I'm told."

Barrent hoped that Myla wouldn't skren any future for him. Life was difficult enough without a mutant's predictions to make it worse.

She was looking up from the faceted glass now, shaking her head sadly. "There's very little I can tell you. I was not able to see the murder performed. But I skrenned a graveyard, and in it I saw your parents' tombstone. It was an old tombstone, perhaps twenty years old. The graveyard was on the outskirts of a place on Earth called Youngerstun."

Barrent reflected a moment, but the name meant nothing to him.

"Also," Myla said, "I skrenned a man who knows about the murder. He can tell you about it, if he will."

"This man saw the murder?"

"Yes."

"Is he the man who informed on me?"

"I don't know," Myla said. "I skrenned the corpse, whose name was Therkaler, and there was a man standing near it. That man's name was Illiardi."

"Is he here on Omega?"

"Yes. You can find him right now in the Euphoriatorium on Little Axe Street. Do you know where that is?"

"I can find it," Barrent said. He thanked the girl and offered payment, which she refused to take. She looked very unhappy. As Barrent was leaving, she called out, "Be careful."

Barrent stopped at the door, and felt an icy chill settle across his chest. "Did you skren my future?" he asked.

"Only a little," Myla said. "Only a few months ahead."

"What did you see?"

"I can't explain it," she said. "What I saw is impossible."

"Tell me what it was."

"I saw you dead. And yet, you weren't dead at all. You were looking at a corpse, which was shattered into shiny fragments. But the corpse was also you."

"What does it mean?"

"I don't know," Myla said.

The Euphoriatorium was a large, garish place which specialized in cut-rate drugs and aphrodisiacs. It catered mostly to a peon and resident clientele. Barrent felt out of status as he shouldered his way through the crowd and asked a waiter where he could find a man named Illiardi.

The waiter pointed. In a corner booth, Barrent saw a bald, thick-shouldered man sitting over a tiny glass of thanapiquita. Barrent went over and introduced himself.

"Pleased to meet you, sir," Illiardi said, showing the obligatory respect of a Second Class Resident for a Privileged Citizen. "How can I be of service?"

"I want to ask you a few questions about Earth," Barrent said.

"I can't remember much about the place," Illiardi said. "But you're welcome to anything I know."

"Do you remember a man named Therkaler?"

"Certainly," Illiardi said. "Thin fellow. Cross-eyed. As mean a man as you could find."

"Were you present when he was killed?"

"I was there. It was the first thing I remembered when I got off the ship."

"Did you see who killed him?"

Illiardi looked puzzled. "I didn't have to see. *I* killed him."

Barrent forced himself to speak in a calm, steady voice. "Are you sure of that? Are you absolutely certain?"

"Of course I'm sure," Illiardi said. "And I'll fight any man who tries to take credit for it. I killed Therkaler, and he deserved worse than that."

"When you killed him," Barrent asked, "did you see *me* anywhere around?"

Illiardi looked at him carefully, then shook his head. "No, I don't think I saw you. But I can't be sure. Right after I killed Therkaler, everything goes sort of blank."

"Thank you," Barrent said. He left the Euphoriatorium.

CHAPTER FOURTEEN

Barrent had much to think about, but the more he thought, the more he became confused. If Illiardi had killed Therkaler, why had Barrent been deported to Omega? If an honest mistake had been made, why hadn't he been released when the true murderer was discovered? Why had someone on Earth accused him of a crime he hadn't committed? And why had a false memory of that crime been superimposed on his mind just beneath the conscious level?

Barrent had no answers for his questions. But he knew that he had never felt like a murderer. Now he had proof, of sorts, that he wasn't a murderer.

The sensation of innocence changed everything for him. He had less tolerance for Omegan ways, and no interest at all in conforming to a criminal mode of life. The only thing he wanted was to escape from Omega and return to his rightful heritage on Earth.

But that was impossible. Day and night, the guardships circled overhead. Even if there had been some way of evading them, escape would still have been impossible. Omegan technology had progressed only as far as the internal combustion engine; the only starships were commanded by Earth forces.

Barrent continued to work in the Antidote Shop, but his lack of public spirit was growing apparent. He ignored invitations from the Dream Shop, and never attended any of the popular public executions. When roving mobs were formed to have a little fun in the Mutant Quarter, Barrent usually pleaded a headache. He never joined the Landing Day Hunts, and he was rude to an accredited salesman from the Torture of the Month Club. Not even visits from Uncle Ingemar could make him change his antireligious ways.

He knew he was asking for trouble. He expected trouble, and the knowledge was strangely exhilarating. After all, there was nothing wrong in breaking the law on Omega—as long as you could get away with it.

WITHIN A month, he had a chance to test his decision. Walking to his shop one day, a man shoved against him in a crowd. Barrent moved away, and the man grabbed him by a shoulder and pulled him around.

"Who do you think you're pushing?" the man asked. He was short and stocky. His clothes indicated Privileged Citizen's rank. Five silver stars on his gunbelt showed his number of authorized kills.

"I didn't push you," Barrent said.

"You lie, you *mutant-lover.*"

The crowd became silent when they heard the deadly insult. Barrent backed away, waiting. The man went for his sidearm in a quick, artistic draw. But Barrent's needlebeam was out a full half-second before the man's weapon had cleared his holster.

He drilled the man neatly between the eyes; then, sensing movement behind him, he swung around.

Two Privileged Citizens were drawing heat guns. Barrent fired, aiming automatically, dodging behind the protection of a shop front. The men crumpled. The wooden front buckled under the impact of a projectile weapon and splinters slashed his hand. Barrent saw a fourth man firing at him from an alley. He brought the man down with two shots.

And that was that. In the space of a few seconds, he had killed four men.

Although he didn't think of himself as having a murderer's mentality, Barrent was pleased and elated. He had fired only in self-defense. He had given the status-seekers something to think about; they wouldn't be so quick to gun for him next time. Quite possibly they would concentrate on easier targets and leave him alone.

When he returned to his shop, he found Joe waiting for him. The little credit thief had a sour look on his face. He said, "I saw your fancy gun-work today. Very pretty."

"Thank you," Barrent said.

"Do you think that sort of thing will help you? Do you think you can just go on breaking the law?"

"I'm getting away with it," Barrent said.

"Sure. But how long do you think you can keep it up?"

"As long as I have to."

"Not a chance," Joe said. "*Nobody* keeps on breaking the law and getting away with it. Only suckers believe that."

"They'd better send some good men after me," Barrent said, reloading his needlebeam.

"That's not how it'll happen," Joe said. "Believe me, Will, there's no counting the ways they have of getting you. Once the law decides to move, there'll be nothing you can do to stop it. And don't expect any help from that girl friend of yours, either."

"Do you know her?" Barrent asked.

"I know everybody," Joe said moodily. "I've got friends in the government. I know that people have had about enough of you. Listen to me, Will. Do you want to end up dead?"

Barrent shook his head. "Joe, can you visit Moera? Do you know how to reach her?"

"Maybe," Joe said. "What for?"

"I want you to tell her something," Barrent said. "I want you to tell her that I didn't commit the murder I was accused of on Earth."

Joe stared at him. "Are you out of your mind?"

"No. I found the man who actually did it. He's a Second Class Resident named Illiardi."

"Why spread it around?" Joe asked. "No sense in losing credit for the kill."

"I didn't murder the man," Barrent said. "I want you to tell Moera. Will you?"

"I'll tell her," Joe said. "If I can locate her. Look, will you remember what I've said? Maybe you still have time to do something about it. Go to Black Mass or something. It might help."

"Maybe I'll do that," Barrent said. "You'll be sure to tell her?"

"I'll tell her," Joe said. He left the Antidote Shop shaking his head sadly.

CHAPTER FIFTEEN

Three days later, Barrent received a visit from a tall, dignified man who stood as rigidly erect as the ceremonial sword that hung by his side. The old man wore a high-collared coat, black pants, and gleaming black boots. From his clothing, Barrent knew he was a high government official.

"The government of Omega sends you greetings," said the official. "I am Norins Jay, Sub-Minister of Games. I am here, as required by law, to inform you personally of your good fortune."

Barrent nodded warily and invited the old man into his apartment. But Jay, erect and proper, preferred to stay in the store.

"The yearly Lottery drawing was held last night," Jay said. "You, Citizen Barrent, are one of the prize winners. I congratulate you."

"What is the prize?" Barrent asked. He had heard of the yearly Lottery, but had only a vague idea of its significance.

"The prize," Jay said, "is honor and fame. Your name inscribed on the civic rolls. Your record of kills preserved for posterity. More concretely, you will receive a new government-issue needlebeam and, afterwards, you will be awarded posthumously the silver sunburst decoration."

"Posthumously?"

"Of course," Jay said. "The silver sunburst is always awarded after death. It is no less an honor for that."

"I'm sure it isn't," Barrent said. "Is there anything else?"

"Just one other thing," Jay said. "As a Lottery winner, you will take part in the symbolic ceremony of the Hunt, which marks the beginning of the yearly Games. The Hunt, as you may know, personifies our Omegan way of life. In the Hunt we see all the complex factors of the dramatic rise and fall from grace, combined with the thrill of the duel and the excitement of the chase. Even peons are allowed to participate in the Hunt, for this is the one holiday open to all, and the one holiday that symbolizes the common man's ability to rise above the restraints of his status."

"If I understand correctly," Barrent said, "I'm one of the people who have been chosen to be hunted."

"Yes," Jay said.

"But you said the ceremony is symbolic. Doesn't that mean no one gets killed?"

"Not at all!" Jay said. "On Omega, the symbol and the thing symbolized are usually one and the same. When we say a Hunt, we mean a true hunt. Otherwise the thing would be mere pageantry."

Barrent stopped a moment to consider the situation. It was not a pleasing prospect. In a man-to-man duel he had an excellent chance of survival. But the yearly Hunt, in which the entire population of Tetrahyde took part, gave him no chance at all. He should have been ready for a possibility like this.

"How was I picked?" he asked.

"By random selection," said Norins Jay. "No other method would be fair to the Hunteds, who give up their lives for Omega's greater glory."

"I can't believe I was picked purely by chance."

"The selection was random," Jay said. "It was made, of course, from a list of suitable victims. Not everyone can be a Quarry in a Hunt. A man must have demonstrated a considerable degree of tenacity and skill before the Games Committee would think of considering him for selection. Being Hunted is an honor; it is not one which we confer lightly."

"I don't believe it," Barrent said. "You people in the government were out to get me. Now, it seems, you've succeeded. It's as simple as that."

"Not at all. I can assure you that none of us in the government bear you the slightest ill will. You may have heard foolish stories about vindictive officials, but they simply aren't true. You have broken the law, but that is no longer the government's concern. Now it is entirely a matter between you and the law."

Jay's frosty blue eyes flashed when he spoke of the law. His back stiffened, and his mouth grew firm.

"The law," he said, "is above the criminal and the judge, and rules them both. The law is inescapable, for an action is either lawful or unlawful. The law, indeed, may be said to have a life of its own, an existence quite apart from the finite lives of the beings who administer it. The law governs every aspect of human behavior; therefore, to the same extent that humans are lawful beings, the law is human. And being human, the law has its idiosyncrasies, just as a man has his. For a citizen who abides by the law, the law is distant and difficult to find. For those who reject and violate it, the law emerges from its musty sepulchers and goes in search of the transgressor."

"And that," Barrent said, "is why I was chosen for the Hunt?"

"Of course," Jay said. "If you had not been chosen in that way, the zealous and never-sleeping law would have selected another means, using whatever instruments were at its disposal."

"Thanks for telling me," Barrent said. "How long do I have before the Hunt begins?"

"Until dawn. The Hunt begins then, and ends at dawn of the following day."

"What happens if I'm not killed?"

Norins Jay smiled faintly. "That doesn't happen often, Citizen Barrent. I'm sure it need not worry you."

"It happens, doesn't it?"

"Yes. Those who survive the Hunt are automatically enrolled in the Games."

"And if I survive the Games?"

"Forget it," Jay said in a friendly manner.

"But what if I do?"

"Believe me, Citizen, you won't."

"I still would like to know what happens if I do."

"Those who live through the Games are beyond the law."

"That sounds promising," Barrent said.

"It isn't. The law, even at its most threatening, is still your guardian. Your rights may be few, but the law guarantees their observance. It is because of the law that I do not kill you here and now." Jay opened his hand, and Barrent saw a tiny single-charge weapon. "The law sets limits, and acts as a modifier upon the behavior of the lawbreaker and the law enforcer. To be sure, the law now states that you must die. But all men must die. The law, by its ponderous and introspective nature, gives you time in which to die. You have a day at least; and without the law, you would have no time at all."

"What happens," Barrent asked, "if I survive the Games and pass beyond the law?"

"There is only one thing beyond the law," Norins Jay said reflectively, "and that is The Black One himself. Those who pass beyond the law belong to him. But it would be better to die a thousand times than to fall living into the hands of The Black One."

Barrent had long ago dismissed the religion of The Black One as superstitious nonsense. But now, listening to Jay's earnest voice, he began to wonder. There might be a difference between the commonplace worship of evil and the actual presence of Evil itself.

"But if you have any luck," Jay said, "you will be killed early. Now I will end the interview with your final instructions."

Still holding the tiny weapon, Jay reached into a pocket with his free hand and withdrew a red pencil. In a quick, practiced motion he drew the pencil over Barrent's cheeks and forehead. He was finished before Barrent had time to recoil.

"That marks you as one of the Hunted," Jay said. "The hunt-marks are indelible. Here is your government-issue needlebeam." He drew a weapon from his pocket and put it on the table. "The Hunt, as I told you, begins at first light of dawn. Anyone may kill you then, except another Hunted man. You may kill in return. But I suggest that you do so with the utmost circumspection. The sound and flash of needlebeams have given many Hunteds away. If you try concealment, be sure you have an exit. Remember that others know Tetrahyde better than you. Skilled Hunters have explored all the possible hiding places over the years; many of the Hunted are trapped during the first hours of the holiday. Good luck, Citizen Barrent."

Jay walked to the door. He opened it and turned to Barrent again.

"There is, I might add, one barely possible way of preserving both life and liberty during the Hunt. But, since it is forbidden, I cannot tell you what it is."

Norins Jay bowed and went out.

BARRENT FOUND, after repeated washings, that the crimson hunt-marks on his face were indeed indelible. During the evening, he disassembled the government-issue needlebeam and inspected its parts. As he had suspected the weapon was defective. He discarded it in favor of his own.

He made his preparations for the Hunt, putting food, water, a coil of rope, a knife, extra ammunition, and a spare needlebeam into a small knapsack. Then he waited, hoping against all reason that Moera and her organization would bring him a last-minute reprieve.

But no reprieve came. An hour before dawn, Barrent shouldered his knapsack and left the Antidote Shop. He had no idea what the other Hunteds were doing; but he had already decided on a place that might be secure from the Hunters.

CHAPTER SIXTEEN

Authorities on Omega agree that a Hunted man experiences a change of character. If he were able to look upon the Hunt as an abstract problem, he might arrive at certain more or less valid conclusions. But the typical Hunted, no matter how great his intelligence, cannot divorce emotion from reasoning. After all, *he* is being hunted. He becomes panic-stricken. Safety seems to lie in distance and depth. He goes as far from home as possible; he goes deep into the ground along the subterranean maze of sewers and conduits. He chooses darkness instead of light, empty places in preference to crowded ones.

This behavior is well known to experienced Hunters. Quite naturally, they look first in the dark, empty places, in the underground passageways, in deserted stores and buildings. Here they find and flush the Hunted with inexorable precision.

Barrent had thought about this. He had discarded his first instinct, which was to hide in the intricate Tetrahyde cloaca. Instead, an hour before dawn, he went directly to the large, brightly lighted building that housed the Ministry of Games.

When the corridors seemed to be deserted, he entered quickly, read the directory, and climbed the stairs to the third floor. He passed a dozen office doors, and finally stopped at the one marked NORINS JAY, SUB-MINISTER OF GAMES. He listened for a moment, then opened the door and stepped in.

There was nothing wrong with old Jay's reflexes. Before Barrent was through the doorway, the old man had spotted the crimson hunt-marks on his face. Jay opened a drawer and reached into it.

Barrent had no desire to kill the old man. He flung the government-issue needlebeam at Jay, and caught him full on the forehead. Jay staggered back against the wall, then collapsed to the floor.

Bending over him, Barrent found that his pulse was strong. He bound and gagged the sub-minister, and pushed him out of sight under his desk. Hunting through the drawers, he found a CONFERENCE: DO NOT DISTURB sign. He hung this outside the door, and locked it. With his own needlebeam drawn, he sat down behind the desk and awaited events.

Dawn came, and a watery sun rose over Omega. From the window, Barrent could see the streets filled with people. There was a hectic carnival atmosphere in the city, and the noise of the holiday celebration was punctuated by the occasional hiss of a beamer or the flat explosion of a projectile weapon.

By noon, Barrent was still undetected. He looked through windows, and found that he had access to the roof. He was glad to have an exit, just as Jay had suggested.

By mid-afternoon, Jay had recovered consciousness. After struggling with his bonds for a while, he lay quietly under the desk.

Just before evening, someone knocked at the door. "Minister Jay, may I come in?"

"Not at the moment," Barrent said, in what he hoped was a fair imitation of Jay's voice.

"I thought you'd be interested in the statistics of the Hunt," the man said. "So far, Citizens have killed seventy-three

Hunteds, with eighteen left to go. That's quite an improvement over last year."

"Yes, it is," Barrent said.

"The percentage who hid in the sewer system was larger this year. A few tried to bluff it out by staying in their homes. We're tracking down the rest in the usual places."

"Excellent," said Barrent.

"None have made the break so far," the man said. "Strange that Hunteds rarely think of it. But of course, it saves us from having to use the machines."

Barrent wondered what the man was talking about. The break? Where was there to break to? And how would machines be used?

"We're already selecting alternates for the Games," the man added. "I'd like to have your approval of the list."

"Use your own judgment," Barrent said.

"Yes, sir," the man said. In a moment, Barrent heard his footsteps moving down the hall. He decided that the man had become suspicious. The conversation had lasted too long, he should have broken it off earlier. Perhaps he should move to a different office.

Before he could do anything, there was a heavy pounding at the door.

"Yes?"

"Citizen's Search Committee," a bass voice answered. "Kindly open the door. We have reason to believe that a Hunted is hiding in there."

"Nonsense," Barrent said. "You can't come in. This is a government office."

"We can," the bass voice said. "No room, office, or building is closed to a Citizen on Hunt Day. Are you opening up?"

Barrent had already moved to the window. He opened it, and heard behind him the sound of men hammering at the door. He fired through the door twice to give them something to think about; then he climbed out through the window.

The rooftops of Tetrahyde, Barrent saw at once, looked like a perfect place for a Hunted; therefore they were the last place a Hunted should be. The maze of closely connected roofs, chimneys, and spires seemed made to order for a chase; but men were already on the roofs. They shouted when they saw him.

Barrent broke into a sprint. Hunters were behind him, and others were closing in from the sides. He leaped a five-foot gap between buildings, managed to hold his balance on a steeply pitched roof, and scrambled around the side.

Panic gave him speed. He was leaving the Hunters behind. If he could keep up the pace for another ten minutes, he would have a substantial lead. He might be able to leave the roofs and find a better place for concealment.

Another five-foot gap between buildings came up. Barrent leaped it without hesitation.

He landed well. But his right foot went completely through rotted shingles, burying itself to the hip. He braced himself and pulled, trying to extricate his leg, but he couldn't get a purchase on the steep, crumbling roof.

"There he is!"

Barrent wrenched at the shingles with both hands. The Hunters were almost within needlebeam distance. By the time he got his leg out, he would be an easy target.

He had ripped a three-foot hole in the roof by the time the Hunters appeared on the next building. Barrent pulled his leg free; then, seeing no alternative, he jumped into the hole.

For a second he was in the air; then he landed feet-first on a table which collapsed under him, spilling him to the floor. He got up and saw that he was in a Hadji-class living room. An old woman sat in a rocking chair less than three feet away. Her jaw was slack with terror; she kept on rocking automatically.

Barrent heard the Hunters crossing to the roof. He went through the kitchen and out the back door, under a tangle of clotheslines and through a small hedge. Someone fired at him from a second-story window. Looking up, he saw a young boy trying to aim a heavy heat beamer. His father had probably forbidden him to hunt in the streets.

Barrent turned into a street, and sprinted until he reached an alley. It looked familiar. He realized that he was in the Mutant Quarter, not far from Myla's house.

He could hear the cries of the Hunters behind him. He reached Myla's house, and found the door unlocked.

They were all together—the one-eyed man, the bald old woman, and Myla. They showed no surprise at his entrance.

"So they picked you in the Lottery," the old man said. "Well, it's what we expected."

Barrent asked, "Did Myla skren it in the water?"

"There was no need to," the old man said. "It was quite predictable, considering the sort of person you are. Bold but not ruthless. That's your trouble, Barrent."

The old man had dropped the obligatory form of address for a Privileged Citizen; and that, under the circumstances, was predictable, too.

"I've seen it happen year after year," the old man said. "You'd be surprised how many promising young men like yourself end up in this room, out of breath, holding a needlebeam as though it weighed a ton with Hunters three minutes behind them. They expect us to help them, but mutants like to stay out of trouble."

"Shut up, Dem," the old woman said.

"I guess we have to help you," Dem said. "Myla's decided on it for reasons of her own." He grinned sardonically. "Her mother and I told her she was wrong, but she insisted. And since she's the only one of us who can skren, we must let her have her own way."

Myla said, "Even with us helping you, there's very little chance that you'll live through the Hunt."

"If I'm killed," Barrent said, "how will your prediction come true? Remember, you saw me looking at my own corpse, and it was in shiny fragments."

"I remember," Myla said. "But your death won't affect the prediction. If it doesn't happen to you in this lifetime, it will simply catch up to you in a different incarnation."

Barrent was not comforted. He asked, "What should I do?"

The old man handed him an armful of rags. "Put these on, and I'll go to work on your face. You, my friend, are going to become a mutant."

IN A short time, Barrent was back on the street. He was dressed in rags. Beneath them he was holding his needlebeam, and in his free hand was a begging cup. The old man had worked lavishly with a pinkish-yellow plastic. Barrent's face was now monstrously swollen at the forehead, and his nose was flat and spread out almost to the cheekbones. The shape of his face had been altered, and the livid hunt-marks were hidden.

A detachment of Hunters raced past, barely giving him a glance. Barrent began to feel more hopeful. He had gained valuable time. The last light of Omega's watery sun was disappearing below the horizon. Night would give him additional opportunities, and with any luck he could elude the Hunters until dawn. After that were the Games, of course; but Barrent wasn't planning on taking part in them. If his disguise was good enough to protect him from an entire hunting city, there was no reason why he should be captured for the Games.

Perhaps, after the holiday was over, he could appear again in Omegan society. Quite possibly if he managed to survive the Hunt and altogether escape the Games, he would be especially rewarded. Such a presumptuous and successful breaking of the law would have to be rewarded...

He saw another group of Hunters coming toward him. There were five in the group, and with them was Tem Rend, looking somber and proud in his new Assassin's uniform.

"You!" one of the Hunters shouted. "Have you seen a Quarry pass this way?"

"No, Citizen," Barrent said, bowing his head respectfully, his needlebeam ready under his rags.

"Don't believe him," a man said. "These damned mutants never tell us a thing."

"Come on, we'll find him," another man said. The group moved away, but Tem Rend stayed behind.

"You sure you haven't seen one of the Hunted go by here?" Rend asked.

"Positive, Citizen," Barrent said, wondering if Rend had recognized him. He didn't want to kill him; in fact, he wasn't sure he could, for Rend's reflexes were uncannily fast. Right now, Rend's needlebeam was hanging loosely from his hand, while Barrent's was already aimed. That split-second advantage might cancel out Rend's superior speed and accuracy. But if it came to conclusions, Barrent thought, it would probably be a tie; in which case, they would more than likely kill each other.

"Well," Rend said, "if you *do* see any of the Hunted, tell them not to disguise themselves as mutants."

"Why not?"

"That trick never works for long," Rend said evenly. "It gives a man about an hour's grace. Then the informers spot him. Now if *I* were being hunted, I might use mutant's disguise. But I wouldn't just sit on a curbstone with it. I'd make a break out of Tetrahyde."

"You would?"

"Most certainly. A few Hunteds every year escape into the mountains. The officials won't talk about it, of course, and most citizens don't know. But the Assassin's Guild keeps complete records of every trick, device, and escape ever used. It's part of our business."

"That's very interesting," Barrent said. He knew that Rend had seen through his disguise. Tem was being a good neighbor—though a bad assassin.

"Of course," Rend said, "it isn't easy to get out of the city. And once a man's out, that doesn't mean he's clear. There are Hunter patrols to watch out for, and even worse than that—"

Rend stopped abruptly. A group of Hunters were coming toward them. Rend nodded pleasantly and walked off.

After the Hunters had passed, Barrent got up and started walking. Rend had given him good advice. Of course some men would escape from the city. Life in Omega's barren mountains would be extremely difficult; but any difficulty was better than death.

If he were able to get by the city gate, he would have to watch for the hunting patrols. And Tem had mentioned something worse. Barrent wondered what that was. Special mountain-trained Hunters, perhaps? Omega's unstable climate? Deadly flora and fauna? He wished Rend had been able to finish the sentence.

By nightfall he had reached the South Gate. Bent painfully over, he hobbled toward the guard detachment that blocked his way out.

CHAPTER SEVENTEEN

There was no trouble with the guards. Whole families of mutants were streaming out of the city, seeking the protection of the mountains until the frenzy of the Hunt was over. Barrent attached himself to one of these groups, and soon he found himself a mile past Tetrahyde, in the low foothills that curled in a semicircle around the city.

The mutants stopped here and made their camp. Barrent went on, and by midnight he was starting up the rocky, windswept slope of one of the higher mountains. He was hungry, but the cool, clear air was exhilarating. He began to believe that he really would live through the Hunt.

He heard a noisy group of Hunters making a sweep around the mountain. He avoided them easily in the darkness, and continued climbing. Soon there was no sound except the steady rush of wind across the cliffs. It was perhaps two in the morning; only three more hours until dawn.

In the small hours of the morning it began to rain, lightly at first, then in a cold torrent. This was predictable weather for Omega. Predictable also were the towering thunderheads that formed over the mountains, the rolling thunder, and the vivid yellow flashes of lightning. Barrent found shelter in a shallow cave, and counted himself lucky that the temperature had not yet plunged.

He sat in the cave, half-dozing, the remnants of his makeup running down his face, keeping a sleepy watch over the slope of the mountain below him. Then, in the brilliant illumination of a lightning flash, he saw something moving up the slope, heading directly toward his cave.

He stood up, the needlebeam ready, and waited for another lightning flash. It came, and now he could see the cold, wet gleam of metal, a flashing of red and green lights, a pair of metal tentacles taking grips on the rocks and small shrubs of the mountainside.

It was a machine similar to the one Barrent had fought in the cellars of the Department of Justice. Now he knew what Rend had wanted to warn him about. And he could see why few of the Hunted escaped, even if they got beyond the city itself. This time, Max would not be operating at random to make a more equal contest out of it. And there would be no exposed fuse box.

As Max came within range, Barrent fired. The blast bounced harmlessly off the machine's armored hide. Barrent left the shelter of his cave and began to climb.

The machine came steadily behind him, up the treacherous wet face of the mountain. Barrent tried to lose it on a plateau of jagged boulders, but Max couldn't be shaken. Barrent realized that the machine must be following a scent of some kind; probably it was keyed to follow the indelible paint on Barrent's face.

On a steep face of the mountain, Barrent rolled boulders onto the machine, hoping he could start an avalanche. Max dodged most of the flying rocks, and let the rest bounce off him, with no visible effect.

At last Barrent was backed into a narrow, steep-sided angle of cliff. He was unable to climb any higher. He waited. When the machine loomed over him, he held the needlebeam against its metal hide and held down the trigger.

Max shuddered for a moment under the impact of the needlebeam's full charge. Then it brushed the weapon away and wrapped a tentacle around Barrent's neck. The metal coils tightened. Barrent felt himself losing consciousness. He had time to wonder whether the coils would strangle him or break his neck.

Suddenly the pressure was gone. The machine had backed away a few feet. Past it, Barrent could see the first gray light of dawn.

He had lived through the Hunt. The machine was not programmed to kill him after dawn. But it wouldn't let him go. It kept him captive in the narrow angle of the cliff until the Hunters came.

They brought Barrent back to Tetrahyde, where a wildly applauding crowd gave him a hero's welcome. After a two-hour procession, Barrent and four other survivors were taken to the office of the Awards Committee. The Chairman made a short and moving speech about the skill and courage each had shown in surviving the Hunt. He gave each of them the rank of Hadji, and presented them with the tiny golden earrings which showed their status.

At the end of the ceremony, the Chairman wished each of the new Hadjis an easy death in the Games.

CHAPTER EIGHTEEN

Guards led Barrent from the office of the Awards Committee. He was brought past a row of dungeons under the Arena, and locked into a cell. The guards told him to be patient; the Games had already begun, and his turn would come soon.

There were nine men crammed into a cell which had been built to hold three. Most of them sat or sprawled in complete and silent apathy, already resigned to their deaths. But one of them was definitely not resigned. He pushed his way to the front of the cell as Barrent entered.

"Joe!"

The little credit thief grinned at him. "A sad place to meet, Will."

"What happened to you?"

"Politics," Joe said. "It's a dangerous business on Omega, especially during the time of the Games. I thought I was safe. But..." He shrugged his shoulders. "I was selected for the Games this morning."

"Is there any chance of getting out of it?"

"There's a chance," Joe said. "I told your girl about you, so perhaps her friends can do something. As for me, I'm expecting a reprieve."

"Is that possible?" Barrent asked.

"Anything is possible. It's better not to hope for it, though."

"What are the Games like?" Barrent asked.

"They're the sort of thing you'd expect," Joe said. "Man-to-man combats, battles against various types of Omegan flora and fauna, needlebeam and heatgun duels. It's all copied from an old Earth festival, I'm told."

"And if anyone survives," Barrent said, "they're beyond the law."

"That's right."

"But what does it mean to be beyond the law?"

"I don't know," Joe said. "Nobody seems to know much about that. All I could find out is, survivors of the Games are taken by The Black One. It's not supposed to be pleasant."

"I can understand that. Very little on Omega *is* pleasant."

"It isn't a bad place," Joe said. "You just haven't the proper spirit of—"

He was interrupted by the arrival of a detachment of guards. It was time for the occupants of Barrent's cell to enter the Arena.

"No reprieve," Barrent said.

"Well, that's how it goes," Joe said.

They were marched out under heavy guard and lined up at the iron door that separated the cell block from the main Arena. Just before the captain of the guards opened the door, a fat, well-dressed man came hurrying down a side corridor waving a paper.

"What's this?" the captain of the guards asked.

"A writ of recognizance," the fat man said, handing his paper to the captain. "On the other side, you'll find a cease-and-desist order." He pulled more papers out of his pockets. "And here is a bankruptcy-transferral notice, a chattel mortgage, a writ of habeas corpus, and a salary attachment."

The captain pushed back his helmet and scratched his narrow forehead. "I can never understand what you lawyers are talking about. What does it mean?"

"It releases him," the fat man said, pointing to Joe.

The captain took the papers, gave them a single puzzled glance, and handed them to an aide. "All right," he said, "take him with you. But it wasn't like this in the old days. *Nothing* stopped the orderly progression of the Games."

Grinning triumphantly, Joe stepped through the ranks of guards and joined the fat lawyer. He asked him, "Do you have any papers for Will Barrent?"

"None," the lawyer said. "His case is in different hands. I'm afraid it might not be completely processed until after the Games are over."

"But I'll probably be dead then," Barrent said.

"That, I can assure you, won't stop the papers from being properly served," the fat lawyer said proudly. "Dead or alive, you will retain all your rights."

The captain of the guards said, "All right, let's go."

"Luck," Joe called out. And then the line of prisoners had passed through the iron door into the glaring light of the Arena.

BARRENT LIVED through the hand-to-hand duels in which a quarter of the prisoners were killed. After that, men armed with swords were matched against the deadlier Omegan fauna. The beasts they fought included the hintolyte and the hintosced—big-jawed, heavily armored monsters whose natural habitat was the desert region far to the south of Tetrahyde. Fifteen men later, these beasts were dead. Barrent was matched with a Saunus, a flying black reptile from the western mountains. For a while he was hard-pressed by this ugly, poison-toothed creature. But in time he figured out a solution. He stopped trying to jab the Saunus's leathery hide and concentrated on severing its broad fan of tailfeathers. When he had succeeded, the Saunus's flying balance was thrown badly off. The reptile crashed into the high wall that separated the combatants from the spectators, and it was relatively easy to administer the final stroke through the Saunus's single huge eye. The vast and enthusiastic crowd in the stadium gave Barrent a lengthy round of applause.

He moved back to the reserve pen and watched other men struggle against the trichomotreds, incredibly fast little creatures the size of rats, with the dispositions of rabid wolverines. It took five teams of prisoners. After a brief interlude of hand-to-hand duelling, the Arena was cleared again.

Now the hard-shelled criatin amphibians lumbered in. Although sluggish in disposition, the criatins were completely protected beneath several inches of shell. Their narrow whiplash tails, which also served them as antennae, were invariably fatal to any man who approached them. Barrent had to fight one of these after it had dispatched four of his fellow prisoners.

He had watched the earlier combats carefully, and had detected the one place where the criatin antennae could not reach. Barrent waited for his chance and jumped for the center of the criatin's broad back.

When the shell split into a gigantic mouth—for this was the criatin method of feeding—Barrent jammed his sword into the opening. The criatin expired with gratifying promptness, and the crowd signified its approval by showering the Arena with cushions.

The victory left Barrent standing alone on the blood-stained sand. The remaining prisoners were either dead or too maimed to fight. Barrent waited, wondering what beast would be next.

A single tendril shot up through the sand, and then another. In seconds, a short, thick tree was growing in the Arena, sending out more roots and tendrils, and pulling all flesh, living or dead, into five small feeding-mouths which circled the base of the trunk. This was the carrion tree, indigenous to the northeastern swamps and imported with great difficulty. It was said to be highly vulnerable to fire; but Barrent had no fire available.

Using his sword two-handed, Barrent lopped off vines; others grew in their place. He worked with frantic speed to keep the vines from surrounding him. His arms were becoming tired, and the tree regenerated faster than he could cut it down. There seemed no way of destroying it.

His only hope lay in the tree's slow movements. These were fast enough, but nothing compared with human musculature. Barrent ducked out of a corner in which the creeping vines were trapping him. Another sword was lying twenty yards away, half-buried in the sand. Barrent reached it, and heard warning shouts from the crowd. He felt a vine close around his ankles.

He hacked at it, and other vines coiled around his waist. He dug his heels into the sand and clashed the swords together, trying to produce a spark.

On his first try, the sword in his right hand broke in half.

Barrent picked up the halves and kept on trying as the vines dragged him closer to the feeding mouths. A shower of sparks flew from the clanging steel. One of them touched a vine.

With incredible suddenness the vine burst into flame. The flame spurted the length of the vine to the main tree system. The five mouths moaned as the fire leaped toward them.

If matters had been left to continue, Barrent would have been burned to death, for the Arena was nearly filled with the highly combustible vines. But the flames were endangering the wooden walls of the Arena. The Tetrahyde guard detachment put the fire out in time to save both Barrent and the spectators.

Swaying with exhaustion, Barrent stood in the center of the Arena, wondering what would be used next against him. But nothing happened. After a moment, a signal was made from the President's box, and the crowd roared in applause.

The Games were over. Barrent had survived.

Still no one left his seat. The audience was waiting to see the final disposition of Barrent, who had passed beyond the law.

He heard a low, reverent gasp from the crowd. Turning quickly, Barrent saw a fiery dot of light appear in mid-air. It swelled, threw out streamers of light, and gathered them in again. It grew rapidly, too brilliant to look upon. And Barrent remembered Uncle Ingemar saying to him, "Sometimes, The Black One rewards us by appearing in the awful beauty of his fiery flesh. Yes, Nephew, I have actually been privileged to see him. Two years ago he appeared at the Games, and he also appeared the year before that…"

The dot became a red and yellow globe about twenty feet in diameter, its lowest curve not quite touching the ground. It grew again. The center of the globe became thinner; a waist appeared, and above the waist the globe turned an impenetrable black. It was two globes now, one brilliant, one dark, joined by a narrow waist. As Barrent watched, the dark globe lengthened and changed into the unforgettable horn-headed shape of The Dark One.

Barrent tried to run, but the huge black-headed figure swept forward and engulfed him. He was trapped in a blinding swirl of radiance, with darkness above it. The light bored into his head, and he tried to scream. Then he passed out.

CHAPTER NINETEEN

Barrent recovered consciousness in a dim, high-ceilinged room. He was lying on a bed. Two people were standing near by. They seemed to be arguing.

"There simply isn't any more time to wait," a man was saying. "You fail to appreciate the urgency of the situation."

"The doctor said he needs at least another three days of rest." It was a woman's voice. After a moment, Barrent realized that Moera was speaking.

"He can have three days."

"And he needs time for indoctrination."

"You told me he was bright. The indoctrination shouldn't take long."

"It might take weeks."

"Impossible. The ship lands in six days."

"Eylan," Moera said, "you're trying to move too fast. We can't do it this time. On the next Landing Day we will be much better prepared—"

"The situation will be out of hand by then," the man said. "I'm sorry, Moera, we have to use Barrent immediately, or not use him at all."

Barrent said, "Use me for what? Where am I? Who are you?"

The man turned to the bed. In the faint light, Barrent saw a very tall, thin, stooped old man with a wispy moustache.

"I'm glad you're awake," he said. "My name is Swen Eylan. I'm in command of Group Two."

"What's Group Two?" Barrent asked. "How did you get me out of the Arena? Are you agents of The Black One?"

Eylan grinned. "Not exactly agents. We'll explain everything to you shortly. First, I think you'd better have something to eat and drink."

A nurse brought in a tray. While Barrent ate, Eylan pulled up a chair and told Barrent about The Black One.

"Our Group," Eylan said, "can't claim to have started the religion of Evil. That appears to have sprung up spontaneously on Omega. But since it was there, we have made occasional use of it. The priests have been remarkably cooperative. After all, the worshipers of Evil set a high positive value upon corruption. Therefore, in the eyes of an Omegan priest, the appearance of a fraudulent Black One is not anathema. Quite the contrary, for in the orthodox worship of Evil, a great deal of emphasis is put upon false images—especially if they are big, fiery, impressive images like the one which rescued you from the Arena."

"How did you produce that?" Barrent asked.

"It has to do with friction surfaces and planes of force," Eylan said. "You'd have to ask our engineers for more details."

"Why did you rescue me?" Barrent asked.

Eylan glanced at Moera, who shrugged her shoulders. Looking uncomfortable, Eylan said, "We'd like to use you for an important job. But before I tell you about it, I think you should know something about our organization. Certainly you must have some curiosity about us."

"A great deal," Barrent said. "Are you some kind of criminal elite?"

"We're an elite," Eylan said, "but we don't consider ourselves criminal. Two entirely different types of people have been sent to Omega. There are the true criminals guilty of murder, arson, armed robbery, and the like. Those are the people you lived among. And there are the people guilty of deviational crimes such as political unreliability, scientific unorthodoxy, and irreligious attitudes. These people compose our organization, which, for the purposes of identification, we call Group Two. As far as we can remember and reconstruct, our crimes were largely a matter of holding different opinions from those which prevailed upon Earth. We were nonconformists. We probably constituted an unstable element, and a threat to the entrenched powers. Therefore we were deported to Omega."

"And you separated yourselves from the other deportees," Barrent said.

"Yes, necessarily. For one thing, the true criminals of Group One are not readily controllable. We couldn't lead them, nor could we allow ourselves to be led by them. But more important than that, we had a job to do that could only be performed in secrecy. We had no idea what devices the guardships employed to watch the surface of Omega. To keep our security intact, we went underground—literally. The room you're in now is about two hundred feet below the surface. We stay out of sight, except for special agents like Moera, who separate the political and social prisoners who belong in Group Two from the others."

"You didn't separate me," Barrent said.

"Of course not. You were allegedly guilty of murder, which put you in Group One. However, your behavior was not typical of Group One. You seemed like good potential material for us, so we helped you from time to time. But we had to be sure of you before taking you into the Group. Your repudiation of the murder charge was strongly in your favor. Also, we questioned Illiardi after you had located him. There seemed no reason to doubt that he performed the murder you were charged with. Even more strongly in your favor were your high survival qualities, which had their ultimate test in the Hunt and the Games. We were badly in need of a man of your abilities."

"Just what is your work?" Barrent asked. "What do you want to accomplish?"

"We want to go back to Earth," Eylan said.

"But that's impossible."

"We don't think so," Eylan said. "We've given the matter considerable study. In spite of the guardships, we think it's possible to return to Earth. We'll find out for certain in six days, when the breakout must be made."

Moera said, "It would be better to wait another six months."

"Impossible. A six months' delay would be ruinous. Every society has a purpose, and the criminal population of Omega is bent upon its own self-destruction. Barrent, you look surprised. Couldn't you see that?"

"I never thought about it," Barrent said. "After all, I was part of it."

"It's self-evident," Eylan said. "Consider the institutions— all centered around legalized murder. The holidays are excuses for mass murders. Even the law, which governs the rate of murder, is beginning to break down. The population lives near the edge of chaos. And rightfully so. There's no longer any security. The only way to live is to kill. The only way to rise in status is to kill. The only safe thing is to kill—more and more, faster and faster."

"You exaggerate," Moera said.

"I don't think so. I realize that there seems to be a certain permanence to Omegan institutions, a certain inherent conservatism even to murder. But it's an illusion. I have no doubt that all dying societies projected their illusion of permanence—right up to the end. Well, the end of Omegan society is rapidly approaching."

"How soon?" Barrent asked.

"An explosion point will be reached in about four months," Eylan said. "The only way to change that would be to give the population a new direction, a different cause."

"Earth," Barrent said.

"Exactly. That's why the attempt must be made immediately."

"Well, I don't know much about it," Barrent said. "But I'll go along with you. I'll gladly be a part of any expedition."

Eylan looked uncomfortable again. "I suppose I haven't made myself clear," he said. "*You* are going to be the expedition, Barrent. You and only you... Forgive me if I've startled you."

CHAPTER TWENTY

According to Eylan, Group Two had at least one serious flaw: the men who composed it were, for the most part, past their physical prime. There were some younger members, of course; but they had had little contact with violence, and little chance to develop traits of self-sufficiency. Secure in the underground, most of them had never fired a beamer in anger, had never been forced to run for their lives, had never encountered the make-or-break situations through which Barrent had lived. They were brave but unproven. They would willingly undertake the expedition to Earth; but they would have little chance of success.

"And you think I would have a chance?" Barrent asked.

"I think so. You're young and strong, reasonably intelligent, and extremely resourceful. You have a high survival quotient. If any man could succeed, I believe you could."

"Why one man?"

"Because there's no sense in sending a group. The chance of detection would simply be increased. By using one man, we get maximum security and opportunity. If you succeed, we will receive valuable information about the nature of the enemy. If you don't succeed, if you are captured, your attempt will be considered the action of an individual rather than a group. We will still be free to start a general uprising from Omega."

"How am I supposed to get back to Earth?" Barrent asked. "Do you have a starship hidden away somewhere?"

"I'm afraid not. We plan to transport you to Earth aboard the next prison ship."

"That's impossible."

"Not at all. We've studied the landings. They follow a pattern. The prisoners are marched out, accompanied by the guards. While they're assembled in the square, the ship itself is undefended, although loosely surrounded by a cordon of guards. To get you aboard, we will start a disturbance. It should take away the guards' attention long enough for you to get on board."

"Even if I succeed, I'll be captured as soon as the guards return."

"You shouldn't be," Eylan said, "The prison ship is an immense structure with many hiding places for a stowaway. And the element of surprise will be in your favor. This may be the first time in the history of Omega that an escape has been attempted."

"And when the ship reaches Earth?"

"You will be disguised as a member of the ship's personnel," Eylan said. "Remember, the inevitable inefficiency of a huge bureaucracy will be working for you."

"I hope so," Barrent said. "Let's suppose I reach Earth safely and get the information you want. How do I send it back?"

"You send it back on the next prison ship," Eylan said. "We plan to capture that one."

Barrent rubbed his forehead wearily. "What makes you think that any of this—my expedition or your uprising—can succeed against an organization as powerful as Earth?"

"We have to take the chance," Eylan said. "Take it or go down in a bloody shambles with the rest of Omega. I agree that the odds are weighted against us. But our choice is either to make the attempt or to die without making any attempt at all."

Moera nodded at this. "Also, the situation has other possibilities. The government of Earth is obviously repressive. That argues the existence of underground resistance groups on Earth itself. You may be able to contact those groups. A revolt both here *and* on Earth would give the government something to think about."

"Maybe," Barrent said.

"We have to hope for the best," Eylan said. "Are you with us?"

"Certainly," Barrent said. "I'd rather die on Earth than on Omega."

"The prison ship lands in six days," Eylan said. "During that time, we will give you the information we have about Earth. Part of it is memory reconstruction, part has been skrenned by the mutants, and the rest is logical constructs. It's all we have, and I think it gives a reasonably accurate picture of current conditions on Earth."

"How soon do we start?" Barrent asked.

"Right now," Eylan said.

BARRENT RECEIVED a general briefing on the physical make-up of Earth, its climate and major population centers. Then he was sent to Colonel Bray, formerly of the Earth Deep Space Establishment. Bray talked to him about the probable military strength of Earth as represented by the number of guardships around Omega and their apparent level of scientific development. He gave estimates of the size of the Earth forces, their probable divisions into land, sea, and space groups, their assumed level of efficiency. An aide, Captain Carell, lectured on special weapons, their probable types and ranges, their availability to the general Earth population. Another aide, Lieutenant Daoud, talked about detection devices, their probable locations, and how to avoid them.

Then Barrent was turned back to Eylan for political indoctrination. From him, Barrent learned that Earth was believed to be a dictatorship. He learned the methods of a dictatorship, its peculiar strengths and weaknesses, the role of the secret police, the use of terror, the problem of informers.

When Eylan was finished with him, Barrent went to a small, beady-eyed man who lectured on Earth's memory-destroying system. Using the premise that memory-destruction was often employed to render opposition ineffective, the man went on to construct the probable nature of an underground movement on Earth given those circumstances, and how Barrent might contact them, and what the underground's capabilities might be.

Finally he was given the full details of Group Two's plan for getting him on board the ship.

When Landing Day came, Barrent felt a definite sense of relief. He was heartily sick of day and night cramming. Any sort of action would seem an improvement.

CHAPTER TWENTY-ONE

Barrent watched the huge prison ship maneuver into position and sink noiselessly to the ground. It gleamed dully in the afternoon sun, tangible proof of Earth's long reach and powerful grasp. A hatch opened, and a landing stage was let down. The prisoners, flanked by guards, marched down and assembled in the square.

As usual, most of the population of Tetrahyde had gathered to watch and cheer the disembarkation ceremony. Barrent moved through the crowd and stationed himself behind the ranks of prisoners and guards. He touched his pocket to make sure the needlebeam was still there. It had been made for him by Group Two fabricators, completely of plastic to escape any metals detector. The rest of his pockets were stuffed with equipment. He hoped he wouldn't have to use any of it.

The loudspeaker voice began to read off the prisoners' numbers, as it had when Barrent had disembarked. He listened, knees slightly bent, waiting for the beginning of the diversion.

The loudspeaker voice was coming to the end of the prisoner list. There were only ten left. Barrent edged forward. The voice droned on. Four prisoners left, three...

As the number of the last prisoner was announced, the diversion began. A black cloud of smoke darkened the pale sky, and Barrent knew that the Group had set fire to the empty barracks in Square A-2. He waited.

Then it came. There was a stupendous explosion, blasting through two rows of empty buildings. The shock wave was staggering. Even before debris began to fall, Barrent was running toward the ship.

The second and third explosions went off as he came into the ship's shadow. Quickly he stripped off his Omegan outer garments. Under them, he wore a facsimile of guard's uniform. Now he ran toward the landing stage.

The loudspeaker voice was calling loudly for order. The guards were still bewildered.

The fourth explosion threw Barrent to the ground. He got to his feet instantly and sprinted up the landing stage. He was inside the ship. Outside, he could hear the guard captain shouting orders. The guards were beginning to form into ranks, their weapons ready to use against the restive crowd. They were retreating to the ship in good order.

Barrent had no more time to listen. He was standing in a long, narrow corridor. He turned to the right and raced toward the bow of the ship. Far behind him, he could hear the heavy marching tread of the guards.

Now, he thought, the information he had been given about the ship had better be right, or the expedition was finished before it began.

He sprinted past rows of empty cells, and came to a door marked GUARD ASSEMBLY ROOM. A lighted green bulb above the door showed that the air system was on. He went by it, and came to another door. Barrent tried it now, and found it unlocked. Within was a room stacked high with spare engine parts. He entered and closed the door.

The guards marched down the corridor. Barrent could hear them talking as they entered the assembly room.

"What do you think started those explosions?"

"Who knows? Those prisoners are crazy, anyhow."

"They'd blow up the whole planet, if they could."

"Good riddance."

"Well, it didn't cause any damage. There was an explosion like that about fifteen years ago. Remember?"

"I wasn't here then."

"Well, it was worse than this. Two guards were killed, and maybe a hundred prisoners."

"What started it?"

"Don't know. These Omegans just enjoy blowing things up."

"Next thing you know, they'll be trying to blow *us* up."

"Not a chance. Not with the guardships up there."

"You think so? Well, I'll be glad to get back to the checkpoint."

"You said it. Be good to get off this ship and live a little."

"It isn't a bad life at the checkpoint, but I'd rather go back to Earth."

"Well, you can't have everything."

The last of the guards entered the assembly room and dogged the door shut. Barrent waited. After a while, he felt the ship vibrate. It was beginning its departure.

He had learned some valuable information. Apparently all or most of the guards got off at the checkpoint. Did that mean that another detachment of guards got on? Probably. And a checkpoint implied that the ship was searched for escaped prisoners. It was probably only a perfunctory search, since no prisoner had escaped in the history of Omega. Still, he would have to figure out a way of avoiding it.

But he would face that when the time came. Now he felt the vibration cease, and he knew that the ship had left the surface of Omega. He was aboard, unobserved, and the ship was on its way to Earth. So far, everything had gone according to plan.

FOR THE next few hours, Barrent stayed in the storage room. He was feeling very tired, and his joints had begun to ache. The air in the small room had a sour, exhausted smell. Forcing himself to his feet, Barrent walked to the air vent and put his hand over it. No air was coming through. He took a small gauge out of his pocket. The oxygen content of the room was falling rapidly.

Cautiously he opened the storeroom door and peered out. Although he was dressed in a perfect replica of guard's uniform, he knew he couldn't pass among men who knew each other so well. He had to stay in hiding. And he had to have air.

The corridors were deserted. He passed the guard assembly room and heard faint murmurs of conversation inside. The green light glowed brightly over the door. Barrent walked on, beginning to feel the first signs of dizziness. His gauge showed him that the oxygen content in the corridor was starting to fall.

The Group had assumed that the air system would be used throughout the ship. Now Barrent could see that, with only guards and crew aboard, there was no need to supply air for the entire ship. There would be air in the little man-inhabited islands of the guardroom and the crew's section, and nowhere else.

Barrent hurried down the dim, silent corridors, gasping for breath. The air was rapidly growing bad. Perhaps it was being used in the assembly room before the ship's main air supply was touched.

He passed unlocked doors, but the green bulbs above them were unlighted. He had a pounding headache, and his legs felt as if they were turning to jelly. He tried to figure out a course of action.

The crew's section seemed to offer him the best chance. Ship's personnel might not be armed. Even if they were, they would be less ready for trouble than the guards. Perhaps he could hold one of the officers at gunpoint; perhaps he could take over the ship.

It was worth trying. It had to be tried.

At the end of the corridor he came to a staircase. He climbed past a dozen deserted levels, and came at last to a stenciled sign on one of the walls. It read CONTROL SECTION, and an arrow pointed the way. Barrent took the plastic needlebeam out of his pocket and staggered down the corridor. He was beginning to lose consciousness. Black shadows formed and dissipated on the edges of his vision. He was experiencing vague hallucinations, flashes of horror in which he felt the corridor walls falling in on him. He found that he was on his hands and knees, crawling toward a door marked CONTROL ROOM—*No Admittance except to Ship's Officers.*

The corridor seemed to be filled with gray fog. It cleared momentarily, and Barrent realized that his eyes were not focusing properly. He pulled himself to his feet and turned the door handle. It began to open. He took a firm grip on the needlebeam and tried to prepare himself for action.

But, as the door opened, darkness closed irrevocably around him. He thought he could see startled faces, hear a voice shouting, "Watch out! He's armed!" And then the blackness closed in completely, and he fell endlessly forward.

CHAPTER TWENTY-TWO

Barrent's return to consciousness was sudden and complete. He sat up and saw that he had fallen inside the control room. The metal door was closed behind him, and he was breathing without difficulty. He could see no sign of the crew. They must have gone after the guards, assuming he would stay unconscious.

He scrambled to his feet, instinctively picking up his needlebeam. He examined the weapon closely, then frowned and put it away. Why, he wondered, would the crew leave him alone in the control room, the most important part of the ship? Why would they leave him armed?

He tried to remember the faces he had seen just before he collapsed. They were indistinct memories, vague and unfocused figures with hollow, dreamlike voices. Had there really been people in here?

The more he thought about it, the more certain he was that he had conjured those people out of his fading consciousness. There had been no one here. He was alone in the ship's nerve center.

He approached the main control board. It was divided into ten stations. Each section had its rows of dials, whose slender indicators pointed to incomprehensible readings. Each had its switches, wheels rheostats, and levers.

Barrent walked slowly past the stations, watching the patterns of flashing lights that ran to the ceiling and rippled along the walls. The last station seemed to be some kind of overall control for the rest. A small screen was marked: *Coordination, Manual/Automatic.* The *Automatic* part was lighted. There were similar screens for navigation, lookout, collision control, subspace entry and exit, normal space entry and exit, and landing. All were automatic. Further on he found the programming screen, which clicked off the progress of the flight in hours, minutes, and seconds. Time to Checkpoint One was now 29 hours, 4 minutes, 51 seconds. Stop-over time, three hours. Time from Checkpoint to Earth, 480 hours.

The control board flashed and hummed to itself, serene and self-sufficient. Barrent couldn't help feeling that the presence of a human in this temple of the machine was sacrilege.

He checked the air ducts. They were set for automatic feed, giving just enough air to support the room's present human population of one.

But where was the crew? Barrent could understand the necessity of operating a starship largely on an automatic programming system. A structure as huge and complex as this had to be self-sufficient. But men had built it, and men had punched out the programs. Why weren't men present to monitor the switchboards, to modify the program when necessary? Suppose the guards had needed more time on Omega? Suppose it became necessary to by-pass the checkpoint and return directly to Earth? Suppose it was imperative to change destination altogether? Who reset the programs, who gave the ship its orders, who possessed the guiding intelligence that directed the entire operation?

Barrent looked around the control room. He found a storage bin filled with oxygen respirators. He put one on, tested it, and went into the corridor.

After a long walk, he reached a door marked CREW'S QUARTERS. Inside, the room was neat and bare. The beds stood in neat rows, without sheets or blankets. There were no clothes in the closets, no personal possessions of any kind. Barrent left and inspected the officers' and captain's quarters. He found no sign of recent human habitation.

He returned to the control room. It was apparent now that the ship had no crew. Perhaps the authorities on Earth felt so certain of their schedules and of the reliability of their ship that they had decided a crew was superfluous. Perhaps...

But it seemed to Barrent a reckless way of doing things. There was something very strange about an Earth that allowed starships to run without human supervision.

He decided to suspend further judgment until he had acquired more facts. For the time being, he had to think about the problems of his own survival. There was concentrated food in his pockets, but he hadn't been able to carry much water. Would the crewless ship have supplies? He had to remember the detachment of guards, down below in their assembly room. And he had to think about what was going to happen at the checkpoint, and what he would do about it.

Barrent found that he did not have to use his own food supplies. In the officers' mess, machines still dispensed food and drink at the push of a button. Barrent didn't know if these were natural or chemically reconstituted foods. They tasted fine and seemed to nourish him, so he really didn't care.

He explored part of the ship's upper levels. After becoming lost several times, he decided not to take any more unnecessary risks. The life-center of the ship was its control room, and Barrent spent most of his time there.

He found a viewport. Activating the switch that opened the shutters, Barrent was able to look out on the vast spectacle of stars glowing in the blackness of space. Stars without end stretched past the furthest limits of his imagination. Looking at this, Barrent felt a strong surge of pride. This was where he belonged, and those unknown stars were his heritage.

The time to the checkpoint dwindled to six hours. Barrent watched new portions of the control board come to life, checking and altering the forces governing the ship, preparing for a landing. Three and a half hours before landing, Barrent made an interesting discovery. He found the central communication system for the entire ship. By turning on the receiving end, he could overhear conversations in the guardroom.

He didn't learn much that was useful to him. Either through caution or lack of concern, the guards didn't discuss politics. Their lives were spent on the checkpoint, except for periods of service on the prison ship. Some of the things they said Barrent found incomprehensible. But he continued to listen, fascinated by anything these men of Earth had to say.

"You ever go swimming in Florida?"

"I never liked salt water."

"The year before I was called to the Guards, I won third prize at the Dayton Orchid Fair."

"I'm buying a retirement villa in Antarctica."

"How much longer for you?"

"Eighteen years."

"Well, someone's got to do it."

"But why me? And why no Earth leaves?"

"You've watched the tapes, you know why. Crime is a disease. It's infectious."

"So what?"

"So if you work around criminals, you run the danger of infection. You might contaminate someone on Earth."

"It isn't fair…"

"Can't be helped. Those scientists know what they're talking about. Besides, checkpoint's not so bad."

"If you like everything artificial…air, flowers, food…"

"Well, you can't have everything. Your family there?"

"They want to get back Earthside."

"After five years on the checkpoint, they say you can't take Earth. The gravity gets you."

"I'll take gravity. Any time…"

From these conversations, Barrent learned that the grim-faced guards were human beings, just like the prisoners on Omega. Most of the guards didn't seem to like the work they were doing. Like Omegans, they longed for a return to Earth.

He stored the information away. The ship had reached the checkpoint, and the giant switchboard flashed and rippled, making its final adjustments for the intricacies of docking.

At last the maneuver was completed and the engines shut down to stand-by. Through the communications system, Barrent heard the guards leave their assembly room. He followed them down the corridors to the landing stage. He heard the last of them, as he left the ship, say, "Here comes the check squad. Whatcha say, boys?"

There was no answer. The guards were gone, and there was a new sound in the corridors: the heavy marching feet of what the guard called the check squad.

There seemed to be a lot of them. Their inspection began in the engine rooms, and moved methodically upward. From the sounds, they seemed to be opening every door on the ship and searching every room and closet.

Barrent held the needlebeam in his perspiring hand and wondered where, in all the territory of the ship, he could hide. He would have to assume that they were going to look everywhere. In that case, his best chance lay in evading them and hiding in a section of the ship already searched.

He slipped a respirator over his head and moved into the corridor.

CHAPTER TWENTY-THREE

Half an hour later, Barrent still hadn't figured out a way of getting past the check squad. They had finished inspecting the lower levels and were moving up to the control room deck. Barrent could hear them marching down the hallways. He kept on walking, a hundred yards in front, trying to find some way of hiding.

There should be a staircase at the end of this passageway. He could take it down to a different level, a part of the ship which had already been searched. He hurried on, wondering if he were wrong about the location of the staircase. He still had only the haziest idea of the layout of the ship. If he were wrong, he would be trapped.

He came to the end of the corridor, and the staircase was there. The footsteps behind him sounded closer. He started down, peering backwards over his shoulder.

And ran headfirst into a man's huge chest.

Barrent flung himself back, bringing his plastic gun to bear on the enormous figure. But he stopped himself from firing. The thing that stood in front of him was not human.

It stood nearly seven feet high, dressed in a black uniform with INSPECTION TEAM—ANDROID B212 stenciled on its front. Its face was a stylization of a human's, cleverly sculptured out of putty-colored plastic. Its eyes glowed a deep, impossible red. It swayed on two legs, balancing carefully, looking at Barrent, moving slowly toward him. Barrent backed away, wondering if a needlebeam could stop it.

He never had a chance to find out, for the android walked past him and continued up the stairs. Stenciled on the back of its uniform were the words RODENT CONTROL DIVISION. This particular android, Barrent realized, was programmed only to look for rats and mice. The presence of a stowaway had made no impression on it. Presumably the other androids were similarly specialized.

He stayed in an empty storage room on a lower level until he heard the sounds of the androids leaving. Then he hurried back to the control room. No guards came aboard. Exactly on schedule, the big ship left the checkpoint. Destination: Earth.

THE REST of the journey was uneventful. Barrent slept and ate and, before the craft entered subspace, watched the endless spectacle of the stars through the viewport. He tried to visualize the planet he was coming to, but no pictures formed in his mind. What sort of a people built huge starships but failed to equip them with a crew? Why did they send out inspection teams, then give those teams the narrowest and most specialized sort of vision? Why did they have to deport a sizable portion of their population—and then fail to control the conditions under which the deportees lived and died? Why was it necessary for them to wipe the prisoners' minds clean of all memory of Earth?

Barrent couldn't think of any answers.

The control room clocks moved steadily on, counting off the minutes and hours of the trip. The ship entered, then emerged from subspace and went into deceleration orbit around a blue and green world which Barrent observed with mixed emotions. He found it hard to realize that he was returning at last to Earth.

CHAPTER TWENTY-FOUR

The starship landed at noon on a brilliant sunlit day, somewhere on Earth's North American continent. Barrent had planned on waiting for darkness before leaving; but the control room screens flashed an ancient and ironic warning: *All passengers and crew must disembark at once. Ship rigged for full decontamination procedure. Twenty minutes.*

He didn't know what was meant by full decontamination procedure. But since the crew was emphatically ordered to leave, a respirator might not provide much safety. Of the two dangers, leaving the ship seemed the lesser.

The members of Group Two had given a good deal of thought to the clothing Barrent would wear upon debarkation. Those first minutes on Earth might be crucial. No cunning could help him if his clothing was obviously strange, outlandish, alien. Typical Earth clothing was the answer; but the Group wasn't sure what the citizens of Earth wore. One part of the Group had wanted Barrent to dress in their reconstructed approximation of civilian dress. Another part felt that the guard's uniform he had worn on board would see him through his arrival on Earth as well. Barrent himself had agreed with a third opinion, which felt that a mechanic's one-piece coverall would be least noticeable around a spacefield, and suffer the least change of style over the years. In the towns and cities, this disguise might put him at a disadvantage; but he had to meet one problem at a time.

He quickly stripped off his guard's uniform. Underneath he wore the lightweight coveralls. His needlebeam concealed, a collapsible lunchbox in his hand, Barrent walked down the corridor to the landing stage. He hesitated for a moment, wondering if he should leave the weapon on the ship. He decided not to part with it. An inspection would reveal him anyhow; with the needlebeam he would have a chance of breaking away from police.

He took a deep breath and marched out of the ship and down the landing stage.

There were no guards, no inspection party, no police, no army units and no customs officials. There was no one at all. Far to one side of the wide field he could see rows of starcraft glistening in the sun. Straight ahead of him was a fence, and in it was an open gate.

Barrent walked across the field, quickly but without obvious haste. He had no idea why it was all so simple. Perhaps the secret police on Earth had more subtle means of checking on passengers from starships.

He reached the gate. There was no one there except a bald, middle-aged man and a boy of perhaps ten. They seemed to be waiting for him. Barrent found it hard to believe that these were government officials; still, who knew the ways of Earth? He passed through the gate.

The bald man, holding the boy by the hand, walked over to him. "I beg your pardon," the man said.

"Yes?"

"I saw you come from the starship. Would you mind if I ask you a few questions?"

"Not at all," Barrent said, his hand near the coverall zipper beneath which lay his needlebeam. He was certain now that the bald man was a police agent. The only thing that didn't make sense was the presence of the child, unless the boy was an agent-in-training.

"The fact of the matter is," the man said, "my boy Ronny here is doing a thesis for his Tenth Grade Master's Degree. On starships."

"So I wanted to see one," Ronny said. He was an undersized child with a pinched, intelligent face.

"He wanted to see one," the man explained. "I told him it wasn't necessary, since all the facts and pictures are in the encyclopedia. But he wanted to see one."

"It gives me a good opening paragraph," Ronny said.

"Of course," Barrent said, nodding vigorously. He was beginning to wonder about the man. For a member of the secret police, he was certainly taking a devious route.

"You work on the ships?" Ronny asked.

"That's right."

"How fast do they go?"

"In real or subspace?" Barrent asked.

This question seemed to throw Ronny off his stride. He pushed out his lower lip and said, "Gee, I didn't know they went in subspace." He thought for a moment. "As a matter of fact, I don't think I know what subspace is."

Barrent and the boy's father smiled understandingly.

"Well," Ronny said, "how fast do they go in real space?"

"A hundred thousand miles an hour," Barrent said, naming the first figure that came into his head.

The boy nodded, and his father nodded. "Very fast," the father said.

"And much faster in subspace of course," Barrent said.

"Of course," the man said. "Starships are very fast indeed. They have to be. Quite long distances involved. Isn't that right, sir?"

"Very long distances," Barrent said.

"How is the ship powered?" Ronny asked.

"In the usual way," Barrent told him. "We had triplex boosters installed last year, but that comes more under the classification of auxiliary power."

"I've heard about those triplex boosters," the man said. "Tremendous things."

"They're adequate," Barrent said judiciously. He was certain now that this man was just what he purported to be: a citizen with no particular knowledge of spacecraft simply bringing his son to the starport.

"How do you get enough air?" Ronny asked.

"We generate our own," Barrent said. "But air isn't any trouble. Water's the big problem. Water isn't compressible, you know. It's hard to store in sufficient quantities. And then there's the navigation problem when the ship emerges from subspace."

"What *is* subspace?" Ronny asked.

"In effect," Barrent said, "it's simply a different level of real space. But you can find all that in your encyclopedia."

"Of course you can, Ronny," the boy's father said. "We mustn't keep the pilot standing here. I'm sure he has many important things to do."

"I *am* rather rushed," Barrent said. "Look around all you want. Good luck on your thesis, Ronny."

Barrent walked for fifty yards, his spine tingling, expecting momentarily to feel the blow of a needlebeam or a shotgun. But when he looked back, the father and son were turned away from him, earnestly studying the great vessel. Barrent hesitated a moment, deeply bothered. So far, the whole thing had been entirely too easy. Suspiciously easy. But there was nothing he could do but go on.

The road from the starport led past a row of storage sheds to a section of woods. Barrent walked until he was out of sight. Then he left the road and went into the woods. He had had enough contact with people for his first day on Earth. He didn't want to stretch his luck. He wanted to think things over, sleep in the woods for the night, and then in the morning go to a city or town.

He pushed his way past dense underbrush into the forest proper. Here he walked through shaded groves of giant oaks. All around him was the chirp and bustle of unseen bird and animal life. Far in front of him was a large white sign nailed to a tree. Barrent reached it, and read: FORESTDALE NATIONAL PARK. PICNICKERS AND CAMPERS WELCOME.

Barrent was a little disappointed, even though he realized that there would be no virgin wilderness so near a starport. In fact, on a planet as old and as highly developed as Earth, there was probably no virgin land at all, except what had been preserved in national forests.

The sun was low on the horizon, and there was a chill in the long shadows thrown across the forest floor. Barrent found a comfortable spot under a gigantic oak, arranged leaves for a bed, and lay down. He had a great deal to think about. Why, for example, hadn't guards been posted at Earth's most important contact point, an interstellar terminus? Did security measures start later at the towns and cities? Or was he already under some sort of surveillance, some infinitely subtle spy system that followed his every movement and apprehended him only when ready? Or was that too fanciful? Could it be that—?

"Good evening," a voice said, close to his right ear.

Barrent flung himself away from the voice in a spasm of nervous reaction, his hand diving for his needlebeam.

"And a very pleasant evening it is," the voice continued, "here in Forestdale National Park. The temperature is seventy-eight point two degrees Fahrenheit, humidity 23 per cent, barometer steady at twenty-nine point nine. Old campers, I'm sure, already recognize my voice. For the new nature-lovers among you, let me introduce myself. I am Oaky, your friendly oak tree. I'd like to welcome all of you, old and new, to your friendly national forest."

Sitting upright in the gathering darkness, Barrent peered around, wondering what kind of a trick this was. The voice really did seem to come from the giant oak tree.

"The enjoyment of nature," said Oaky, "is now easy and convenient for everyone. You can enjoy complete seclusion and still be no more than a ten-minute walk from public transportation. For those who do not desire seclusion, we have guided tours at nominal cost through these ancient glades. Remember to tell your friends about your friendly national park.

The full facilities of this park are waiting for all lovers of the great outdoors."

A panel in the tree opened. Out slid a bedroll, a Thermos bottle, and a box supper.

"I wish you a pleasant evening," said Oaky, "amid the wild splendor of nature's wonderland. And now the National Symphony Orchestra under the direction of Otter Krug brings you 'The Upland Glades,' by Ernesto Nestrichala, recorded by the National North American Broadcasting Company. This is your friendly oak tree signing off."

Music emanated from several hidden speakers. Barrent scratched his head; then, deciding to take matters as they came, he ate the food, drank coffee from the Thermos, unrolled the bedroll, and lay down.

Sleepily he contemplated the notion of a forest wired for sound, equipped with food and drink, and none of it more than ten minutes from public transportation. Earth certainly did a lot for her citizens. Presumably they liked this sort of thing. Or did they? Could this be some huge and subtle trap which the authorities had set for him?

He tossed and turned for a while, trying to get used to the music. After a while it blended into the background of windblown leaves and creaking branches. Barrent went to sleep.

CHAPTER TWENTY-FIVE

In the morning, the friendly oak tree dispensed breakfast and shaving equipment. Barrent ate, washed and shaved, and set out for the nearest town. He had his objectives firmly in mind. He had to establish some sort of foolproof disguise, and he had to make contact with Earth's underground. When this was accomplished, he had to find out as much as he could about Earth's secret police, military dispositions, and the like.

Group Two had worked out a procedure for accomplishing these objectives. As Barrent came to the outskirts of a town, he hoped that the Group's methods would work. So far, the Earth he was on had very little resemblance to the Earth which the Group had reconstructed.

He walked down interminable streets lined with small white cottages. At first, he thought every house looked the same. Then he realized that each had one or two small architectural differences. But instead of distinguishing the houses, these niggling differences simply served to point up the monotonous similarities. There were hundreds of these cottages, stretching as far as he could see, each of them set upon a little plot of carefully tended grass. Their genteel sameness depressed him. Unexpectedly he missed the ridiculous, clumsy, make-shift individuality of Omegan buildings.

He reached a shopping center. The stores repeated the pattern set by the houses. They were low, discreet, and very similar. Only a close inspection of window displays revealed differences between a food store and a sports shop. He passed a small building with a sign that read, ROBOT CONFESSIONAL—*Open 24 hours a day.* It seemed to be some sort of church.

The procedure set by Group Two for locating the underground on Earth was simple and straightforward. Revolutionaries, he had been told, are found in greatest quantity among a civilization's most depressed elements. Poverty breeds dissatisfaction; the have-nots want to take from those who have. Therefore, the logical place to look for subversion is in the slums.

It was a good theory. The trouble was, Barrent couldn't find any slums. He walked for hours, past neat stores and pleasant little homes, playgrounds and parks, scrupulously tended farms, and then past more houses and stores. Nothing looked much better or worse than anything else.

By evening, he was tired and footsore. As far as he could tell, he had discovered nothing of significance. Before he could penetrate any deeper into the complexities of Earth, he would have to question the local citizens. It was a dangerous step, but one which he could not avoid.

He stood near a clothing store in the gathering dusk and decided upon a course of action. He would pose as a foreigner, a man newly arrived in North America from Asia or Europe. In that way, he should be able to ask questions with a measure of safety.

A man was walking toward him, a plump, ordinary-looking fellow in a brown business tunic. Barrent stopped him. "I beg your pardon," he said. "I'm a stranger here, just arrived from Rome."

"Really?" the man said.

"Yes. I'm afraid I don't understand things over here very well," Barrent said, with an apologetic little laugh. "I can't seem to find any cheap hotels. If you could direct me—"

"Citizen, do you feel all right?" the man asked, his face hardening.

"As I said, I'm a foreigner, and I'm looking—"

"Now look," the man said, "you know as well as I do that there aren't any outlanders any more."

"There aren't?"

"Of course not. I've *been* in Rome. It's just like here in Wilmington. Same sort of houses and stores. No one's an outlander any more."

Barrent couldn't think of anything to say. He smiled nervously.

"Furthermore," the man said, "there are no cheap lodgings anywhere on Earth. Why should there be? Who would stay in them?"

"Who indeed?" Barrent said. "I guess I've had a little too much to drink."

"No one drinks any more," the man said. "I don't understand. What sort of a game is this?"

"What sort of a game do you *think* it is?" Barrent asked, falling back on a technique which the Group had recommended.

The man stared at him, frowning. "I think I get it," he said. "You must be an Opinioner."

"Mmm," Barrent said, noncommittally.

"Sure, that's it," the man said. "You're one of those citizens goes around asking people's opinions. For surveys and that sort of thing. Right?"

"You've made a very intelligent guess," Barrent said.

"Well, I don't suppose it was too hard. Opinioners are always walking around trying to get people's attitudes on things. I would have spotted you right away if you'd been wearing Opinioners' clothing." The man started to frown again. "How come you aren't dressed like an Opinioner?"

"I just graduated," Barrent said. "Haven't had a chance to get the clothes."

"Oh. Well, you should get the proper wear," the man said sententiously. "How can a citizen tell your status?"

"Just a test sampling," Barrent said. "Thank you for your cooperation, sir. Perhaps I'll have a chance to interview you again in the near future."

"Any time," the man said. He nodded politely and walked off.

Barrent thought about it, and decided that the occupation of Opinioner was perfect for him. It would give him the all-important right to ask questions, to meet people, to find out how Earth lived. He would have to be careful, of course, not to reveal his ignorance. But working with circumspection, he should have a general knowledge of this civilization in a few days.

First, he would have to buy Opinioners' clothing. That seemed to be important. The trouble was, he had no money with which to pay for it. The Group had been unable to duplicate Earth money; they couldn't even remember what it looked like.

But they had provided him with a means of overcoming even that obstacle. Barrent turned and went into the nearest costumer's.

The proprietor was a short man with china-blue eyes and a salesman's ready smile. He welcomed Barrent and asked how he could be of service.

"I need Opinioners' clothing," Barrent told him. "I've just graduated."

"Of course, sir," the owner said. "And you've come to the right place for it. Most of the smaller stores don't carry the clothing for anything but the more...ah...common professions. But here at Jules Wonderson's, we have ready-wears for all of the five hundred and twenty major professions listed in the Civil Status Almanac. I am Jules Wonderson."

"A pleasure," Barrent said. "Have you a ready-wear in my size?"

"I'm sure I have," Wonderson said. "Would you care for a Regular or a Special?"

"A Regular will do nicely."

"Most new Opinioners prefer the Special," Wonderson said. "The little extra simulated handmade touches increase the public's respect."

"In that case I'll take the Special."

"Yes, sir. Though if you could wait a day or two, we will be having in a new fabric—a simulated Home Loom, complete with natural weaving mistakes. For the man of status discrimination. A real prestige item."

"Perhaps I'll come back for that," Barrent said. "Right now, I need a ready-wear."

"Of course, sir," Wonderson said, disappointed but hiding it bravely. "If you'll wait just one little minute..."

After several fittings, Barrent found himself wearing a black business suit with a thin edge of white piping around the lapels. To his inexperienced eye it looked almost exactly like the other suits Wonderson had on display for bankers, stock brokers, grocers, accountants, and the like. But for Wonderson, who talked about the banker's lapel and the insurance agent's drape, the differences were as clear as the gross status-symbols of Omega. Barrent decided it was just a question of training.

"There, sir!" Wonderson said. "A perfect fit, and a fabric guaranteed for a lifetime. All for thirty-nine ninety-five."

"Excellent," Barrent said. "Now, about the money—"

"Yes, sir?"

Barrent took the plunge. "I haven't any."

"You haven't, sir? That's quite unusual."

"Yes, it is," Barrent said. "However, I *do* have certain articles of value." From his pocket he took three diamond rings with which the Group on Omega had supplied him. "These stones are genuine diamonds, as any jeweler will be glad to attest. If you would take one of them until I have the money for payment—"

"But, sir," Wonderson said, "diamonds and such have no intrinsic value. They haven't since '23, when Von Blon wrote the definitive work destroying the concept of scarcity value."

"Of course," Barrent said, at a loss for words.

Wonderson looked at the rings. "I suppose these have a sentimental value, though."

"Certainly. We've had them in the family for generations."

"In that case," Wonderson said, "I wouldn't want to deprive you of them. Please, no arguments, sir! Sentiment is the most priceless of emotions. I couldn't sleep nights if I took even one of these family heirlooms from you."

"But there's the matter of payment."

"Pay me at your leisure."

"You mean you'll trust me, even though you don't know me?"

"Most certainly," Wonderson said. He smiled archly. "Trying out your Opinioner's methods, aren't you? Well, even a child knows that our civilization is based upon trust, not collateral. It is axiomatic that even a stranger is to be trusted until he has conclusively and unmistakably proven otherwise."

"Haven't you ever been cheated?"

"Of course not. Crime is nonexistent these days."

"In that case," Barrent asked, "what about Omega?"

"I beg your pardon?"

"Omega, the prison planet. You must have heard of it."

"I think I have," Wonderson said cautiously. "Well, I should have said that crime is *almost* nonexistent. I suppose there will always be a few congenital criminal types, easily recognizable as such. But I'm told they don't amount to more than ten or twelve individuals a year out of a population of nearly two billion." He smiled broadly. "My chances of meeting one are exceedingly rare."

Barrent thought about the prison ships constantly shuttling back and forth between Earth and Omega, dumping their human cargo and returning for more. He wondered where Wonderson got his statistics. For that matter, he wondered where the police were. He had seen no military uniform since leaving the starship. He would have liked to ask about it, but it seemed wiser to discontinue that line of questioning.

"Thank you very much for the credit," Barrent said. "I'll be back with the payment as soon as possible."

"Of course you will," Wonderson said, warmly shaking Barrent's hand. "Take your time, sir. No rush at all."

Barrent thanked him again and left the store.

He had a profession now. And if other people believed as Wonderson did, he had unlimited credit. He was on a planet that seemed, at first glance, to be a utopia. The utopia presented certain contradictions, of course. He hoped to find out more about them over the next few days.

Down the block, Barrent found a hotel called The Bide-A-Bit. He engaged a room for the week, on credit.

CHAPTER TWENTY-SIX

In the morning, Barrent asked directions to the nearest branch of the public library. He decided that he needed as much background out of books as he could get. With a knowledge of the history and development of Earth's civilization, he would have a better idea of what to expect and what to watch out for.

His Opinioner's clothing allowed him access to the closed shelves where the history books were kept. But the books themselves were disappointing. Most of them were Earth's ancient history, from earliest beginnings to the dawn of atomic power. Barrent skimmed through them. As he read, some memories of prior reading returned to him. He was able to jump quickly from Periclean Greece to Imperial Rome, to Charlemagne and the Dark Ages, from the Norman Conquest to the Thirty Years' War, and then to a rapid survey of the Napoleonic Era. He read with more care about the World Wars. The book ended with the explosion of the first atom bombs. The other books on the shelf were simply amplifications of various stages of history he had found in the first book.

After a great deal of searching, Barrent found a small work entitled, "The Postwar Dilemma, Volume 1," by Arthur Whittler. It began where the other histories had left off; with the atomic bombs exploding over Hiroshima and Nagasaki. Barrent sat down and began to read carefully.

He learned about the Cold War of the 1950's, when several nations were in possession of atomic and hydrogen weapons. Already, the author stated, the seeds of a massive and stultifying conformity were present in the nations of the world. In America, there was the frenzied resistance to communism. In Russia and China, there was the frenzied resistance to capitalism. One by one, all the nations of the world were drawn into one camp or the other. For purposes of internal security, all countries relied upon the newest propaganda and indoctrination techniques. All countries felt they needed, for survival's sake, a rigid adherence to state-approved doctrines.

The pressure upon the individual to conform became both stronger and subtler.

The dangers of war passed. The many societies of Earth began to merge into a single superstate. But the pressure to conform, instead of lessening, grew more intense. The need was dictated by the continued explosive increase in population, and the many problems of unification across national and ethnic lines. Differences in opinion could be deadly; too many groups now had access to the supremely deadly hydrogen bombs.

Under the circumstances, deviant behavior could not be tolerated.

Unification was finally completed. The conquest of space went on, from moon ship to planet ship to star ship. But Earth became increasingly rigid in its institutions. A civilization more inflexible than anything produced by medieval Europe punished any opposition to existing customs, habits, beliefs. These breaches of the social contract were considered major crimes as serious as murder or arson. They were punished similarly. The antique institutions of secret police, political police, informers, all were used. Every possible device was brought to bear toward the all-important goal of conformity.

For the nonconformists, there was Omega.

Capital punishment had been banished long before, but there was neither room nor resources to take the growing number of criminals who crammed prisons everywhere. The world leaders finally decided to transport these criminals to a separate prison world, copying a system which the French had used in Guiana and New Caledonia, and the British had used in Australia and early North America. Since it was impossible to rule Omega from Earth, the authorities didn't try. They simply made sure that none of the prisoners escaped.

That was the end of volume one. A note at the end said that volume two was to be a study of contemporary Earth. It was entitled *The Status Civilization*.

The second volume was not on the shelves. Barrent asked the librarian, and was told that it had been destroyed in the interests of public safety.

Barrent left the library and went to a little park. He sat and stared at the ground and tried to think.

He had expected to find an Earth similar to the one described in Whittler's book. He had been prepared for a police state, tight security controls, a repressed populace, and a growing air of unrest. But that, apparently, was the past. So far, he hadn't even seen a policeman. He had observed no security controls, and the people he had met did not seem harshly repressed. Quite the contrary. This seemed like a completely different world...

Except that year after year, the ships came to Omega with their cargoes of brainwashed prisoners. Who arrested them? Who judged them? What sort of a society produced them?

He would have to find out the answers himself.

CHAPTER TWENTY-SEVEN

Early the next morning, Barrent began his exploration. His technique was simple. He rang doorbells and asked questions. He warned all his subjects that his real questions might be interspersed with tricks or nonsense questions, whose purpose was to test the general awareness level. In that way, Barrent found he could ask anything at all about Earth, could explore controversial or even nonexistent areas, and do so without revealing his own ignorance.

There was still the danger that some official would ask for his credentials, or that the police would mysteriously spring up when least expected. But he had to take those risks. Starting at the beginning of Orange Esplanade, Barrent worked his way northward, calling at each house as he went. His results were uneven, as a selective sampling of his work shows:

(*Citizen A. L. Gotthreid, age 55, occupation home-tender. A strong, erect woman, imperious but polite, with a no-nonsense air about her.*)

"You want to ask me about class and status? Is that it?"

"Yes, ma'am."

"You Opinioners are *always* asking about class and status. One would think you'd know all about it by now. But very well. Today, since everyone is equal, there is only one class. The *middle* class. The only question then is—to what portion of the middle class does one belong? High, low, or middle?"

"And how is that determined?"

"Why, by all sorts of things. The way a person speaks, eats, dresses, the way he acts in public. His manners. His clothing.

You can always tell your upper middle class man by his clothes. It's quite unmistakable."

"I see. And the lower middle classes?"

"Well, for one thing they lack creative energy. They wear ready-made clothing, for example, without taking the trouble to improve upon it. The same goes for their homes. Mere uninspired adornment won't do, let me add. That's simply the mark of the *nouveau* upper middle class. One doesn't receive such persons in the home."

"Thank you, Citizen Gotthreid. And where would you classify yourself statuswise?"

(With the very faintest hesitation). "Oh, I've never thought much about it—upper middle, I suppose."

(*Citizen Dreister, age 43, occupation shoe vendor. A slender, mild man, young-looking for his years.*)

"Yes, sir. Myra and I have three children of school age. All boys."

"Could you give me some idea what their education consists of?"

"They learn how to read and write, and how to become good citizens. They're already starting to learn their trades. The oldest is going into the family business—shoes. The other two are taking apprenticeship courses in groceries and retail marketing. That's my wife's family's business. They also learn how to retain status, and how to utilize standard techniques for moving upward. That's about what goes on in the open classes."

"Are there other school classes which are not open?"

"Well, naturally there are the closed classes. Every child attends them."

"And what do they learn in the closed classes?"

"I don't know. They're closed, as I said."

"Don't the children ever speak about those classes?"

"No. They talk about everything under the sun, but not about that."

"Haven't you any idea what goes on in the closed classes?"

"Sorry, I don't. At a guess—and it's only a guess, mind you—I'd say it's probably something religious. But you'd have to ask a teacher for that."

"Thank you, sir. And how do you classify yourself statuswise?"

"Middle middle class. Not much doubt about that."

(*Citizen Maryjane Morgan, age 51, occupation school-teacher. A tall, bony woman.*)

"Yes, sir, I think that just about sums up our curriculum at the Little Beige Schoolhouse."

"Except for the closed classes."

"I beg your pardon, sir?"

"The closed classes. You haven't discussed those."

"I'm afraid I can't."

"Why not, Citizen Morgan?"

"Is this a trick question? Everyone knows that teachers aren't allowed in the closed classes."

"Who *is* allowed in?"

"The children, of course."

"But who teaches them?"

"The government is in charge of that."

"Of course. But who, specifically, does the teaching in the closed classes?"

"I have no idea, sir. It's none of my business. The closed classes are an ancient and respected institution. What goes on in them is quite possibly of a religious nature. But that's only a guess. Whatever it is, it's none of my business. Nor is it yours, young man, Opinioner or not."

"Thank you, Citizen Morgan."

(*Citizen Edgar Nief, age 107, occupation retired officer. A tall, stooped man with cane, icy blue eyes undimmed by age.*)

"A little louder, please. What was that question again?"

"About the armed forces. Specifically I asked—"

"I remember now. Yes, young man, I was a colonel in the Twenty-first North American Spaceborne Commando, which was a regular unit of the Earth Defense Corps."

"And did you retire from the service?"

"No, the service retired from me."

"I beg pardon, sir?"

"You heard me correctly, young man. It happened just sixty-three years ago. The Earth Armed Forces were demobilized, except for the police whom I cannot count. But all regular units were demobilized."

"Why was that done, sir?"

"There wasn't anyone to fight. Wasn't even anyone to guard against, or so I was told. Damned foolish business, I say."

"Why, sir?"

"Because an old soldier knows that you can never tell when an enemy might spring up. It could happen now. And then where would we be?"

"Couldn't the armies be formed again?"

"Certainly. But the present generation has no concept of serving under arms. There are no leaders left, outside of a few useless old fools like me. It would take years for an effective force, effectively led, to be formed."

"And in the meantime, Earth is completely open to invasion from the outside?"

"Yes, except for the police units. And I seriously doubt their reliability under fire."

"Could you tell me about the police?"

"There is nothing I know about them. I have never bothered my head about non-military matters."

"But it is conceivable that the police have now taken over the functions of the army, isn't it? That the police constitute a sizable and disciplined paramilitary force?"

"It is possible, sir. Anything is possible."

(Citizen Moertin Honners, age 31, occupation verbalizer. A slim, languid man with an earnest, boyish face and smooth, corn-blond hair.)

"You are a verbalizer, Citizen Honners?"

"I am, sir. Though perhaps 'author' would be a better word, if you don't mind."

"Of course. Citizen Honners, are you presently engaged in writing for any of the periodicals I see on the dissemination stands?"

"Certainly not! These are written by incompetent hacks for the dubious delectation of the lower middle class. The stories, in case you didn't know, are taken line by line from the works of various popular writers of the twentieth and twenty-first centuries. The people who do the work merely substitute adjectives and adverbs. Occasionally, I'm told, a more daring hack will substitute a verb, or even a noun. But that is rare. The editors of such periodicals frown upon sweeping innovations."

"And you are not engaged in such work?"

"Absolutely not! My work is noncommercial. I am a Creative Conrad Specialist."

"Would you mind telling me what that means, Citizen Honners?"

"I'd be happy to. My own particular field of endeavor lies in re-creating the works of Joseph Conrad, an author who lived in the pre-atomic era."

"How do you go about re-creating those works, sir?"

"Well, at present I am engaged in my fifth re-creation of *Lord Jim*. To do it, I steep myself as thoroughly as possible in the original work. Then I set about rewriting it as Conrad would have written it if he had lived today. It is a labor which calls for extreme diligence, and for the utmost in artistic integrity. A single slip could mar the re-creation. As you can see, it calls for a preliminary mastery of Conrad's vocabulary, themes, plots, characters, mood, approach, and so on. All this goes in, and yet the book cannot be a slavish *repeat*. It must have something new to say, just as Conrad would have said it."

"And have you succeeded?"

"The critics have been generous, and my publisher gives me every encouragement."

"When you have finished your fifth re-creation of *Lord Jim*, what do you plan to do?"

"First I shall take a long rest. Then I shall re-create one of Conrad's minor works. *The Planter of Malata*, perhaps."

"I see. Is re-creation the rule in all the arts?"

"It is the goal of the true aspiring artist, no matter what medium he has chosen to work in. Art is a cruel mistress, I fear."

(*Citizen Willis Ouerka, age 8, occupation student. A cheerful, black-haired, sun-tanned boy.*)

"I'm sorry, Mr. Opinioner, my parents aren't home right now."

"That's perfectly all right, Willis. Do you mind if I ask you a question or two?"

"I don't mind. What's that you got under your jacket, Mister? It bulges."

"I'll ask the questions, Willis, if you don't mind... Now, do you like school?"

"It's all right."

"What courses do you take?"

"Well, there's reading and writing and status appreciation, and courses in art, music, architecture, literature, ballet, and theater. The usual stuff."

"I see. That's in the open classes?"

"Sure."

"Do you also attend a closed class?"

"Sure I do. Every day."

"Do you mind talking about it?"

"I don't mind. Is that bulge a gun? I know what guns are. Some of the big boys were passing around pictures at lunchtime a couple days ago and I peeked. Is it a gun?"

"No. My suit doesn't fit very well, that's all. Now then. Would you mind telling me what you do in the closed class?"

"I don't mind."

"What happens, then?"

"I don't remember."

"Come now, Willis."

"Really, Mr. Opinioner. We all go into this classroom, and we come out two hours later for recess. But that's all. I can't remember anything else. I've talked with the other kids. They can't remember either."

"Strange…"

"No, sir. If we were supposed to remember, it wouldn't be *closed*."

"Perhaps so. Do you remember what the room looks like, or who your teacher is for the closed class?"

"No, sir. I really don't remember anything at all about it."

"Thank you. Willis."

(*Citizen Cuchulain Dent, age 37, occupation inventor. A prematurely bald man with ironic, heavy-lidded eyes.*)

"Yep, that's right. I'm an inventor specializing in games. I brought out *Triangulate—Or Else!* last year. It's been pretty popular. Have you seen it?"

"I'm afraid not."

"Sort of a cute game. It's a simulated lost-in-space thing. The players are given incomplete data for their miniature computers, additional information as they win it. Space hazards for penalties. Lots of flashing lights and stuff like that. Very big seller."

"Do you invent anything else, Citizen Dent?"

"When I was a kid, I worked up an improved seeder harvester. Designed to be approximately three times as efficient as the present models. And would you believe it, I really thought I had a chance of selling it."

"Did you sell it?"

"Of course not. At that time I didn't realize that the patent office was closed permanently except for the games section."

"Were you angry about that?"

"A little angry at the time. But I soon realized that the models we have are plenty good enough. There's no need for more efficient or more ingenious inventions. Folks today are satisfied with what they've got. Besides, new inventions would be of no service to mankind. Earth's birth and death rate are stable, and there's enough for everyone. To produce a new invention, you'd have to retool an entire factory. That would be almost impossible, since all the factories today are automatic and self-repairing. That's why there's a moratorium on invention, except in the novelty game field."

"How do you feel about it?"

"What's there to feel? That's how things are."

"Would you like to have things different?"

"Maybe. But being an inventor, I'm classified as a potentially unstable character anyhow."

(*Citizen Barn Threnten, age 41, occupation atomics engineer specializing in spacecraft design. A nervous, intelligent-looking man with sad brown eyes.*)

"You want to know what I do in my job? I'm sorry you asked that, Citizen, because I don't do a thing except walk around the factory. Union rules require one stand-by human for every robot or robotized operation. That's what I do. I just stand by."

"You sound dissatisfied, Citizen Threnten."

"I am. I wanted to be an atomics engineer. I trained for it. Then when I graduated, I found out my knowledge was fifty years out of date. Even if I learned what was going on now, I'd have no place to use it."

"Why not?"

"Because everything in atomics is automatized. I don't know if the majority of the population knows that, but it's true. From raw material to finished product, it's all completely automatic. The only human participation in the program is quantity-control in terms of population indexes. And even that is minimal."

"What happens if a part of an automatic factory breaks down?"

"It gets fixed by robot repair units."

"And if they break down?"

"The damned things are self-repairing. All I can do is stand by and watch, and fill out a report. Which is a ridiculous position for a man who considers himself an engineer."

"Why don't you turn to some other field?"

"No use. I've checked, and the rest of the engineers are in the same position I'm in, watching automatic processes which they don't understand. Name your field: food processing, automobile manufacture, construction, biochem., it's all the same. Either stand-by engineers or no engineers at all."

"This is true for spaceflight also?"

"Sure. No member of the spacepilot's union has been off Earth for close to fifty years. They wouldn't know how to operate a ship."

"I see. All the ships are set for automatic."

"Exactly. Permanently and irrevocably automatic."

"What would happen if these ships ran into an unprecedented situation?"

"That's hard to say. The ships can't think, you know; they simply follow pre-set programs. If the ships ran into a situation for which they were not programmed, they'd be paralyzed, at least temporarily. I think they have an optimum-choice selector which is supposed to take over unstructured situations; but it's never been tried out. At best, it would react sluggishly. At worst, it wouldn't work at all. And that would be fine by me."

"Do you really mean that?"

"I certainly do. I'm sick of standing around watching a machine do the same thing day after day. Most of the professional men I know feel the same way. We want to do something. Anything. Did you know that a hundred years ago human-piloted starships were exploring the planets of other solar systems?"

"Yes."

"Well, that's what we should be doing now. Moving outward, exploring, advancing. That's what we need."

"I agree. But don't you think you're saying rather dangerous things?"

"I know I am. But frankly, I just don't care any longer. Let them ship me to Omega if they want to. I'm doing no good here."

"Then you've heard about Omega?"

"Anyone connected with starships knows about Omega. Round trips between Omega and Earth, that's all our ships do. It's a terrible world. Personally, I put the blame on the clergy."

"The clergy?"

"Absolutely. Those sanctimonious fools with their endless drivel about the Church of the Spirit of Mankind Incarnate. It's enough to make a man wish for a little evil..."

(*Citizen Father Boeren, age 51, occupation clergyman. A stately, plum-shaped man wearing a saffron robe and white sandals.*)

"That's right, my son, I am the abbot of the local branch of the Church of the Spirit of Mankind Incarnate. Our church is the official and exclusive religious expression of the government of Earth. Our religion speaks for all the peoples of Earth. It is a composite of the best elements of all the former religions, both major and minor, skillfully blended into a single all-embracing faith."

"Citizen Abbot, aren't there bound to be contradictions in doctrine among the various religions which make up your faith?"

"There *were*. But the forgers of our present Church threw out all controversial matter. We wanted agreement, not dissension. We preserve only certain colorful facets of those early great religions; facets with which people can identify. There have never been any schisms in our religion, because we are all-acceptant. One may believe anything one wishes, as long as it preserves the holy spirit of Mankind Incarnate. For our worship, you see, is the true worship of Man. And the spirit we recognize is the spirit of the divine and holy Good."

"Would you define Good for me, Citizen Abbot?"

"Certainly. Good is that force within us which inspires men to acts of conformity and subservience. The worship of Good is essentially the worship of oneself, and therefore the only true worship. The self which one worships is the ideal social being: the man content in his niche in society, yet ready to creatively advance his status. Good is gentle, since it is a true reflection of the loving and pitying universe. Good is continually changing in its aspects, although it comes to us in the... You have a strange look on your face, young man."

"I'm sorry, Citizen Abbot. I believe I heard that sermon, or one very much like it."

"It is true wherever one hears it."

"Of course. One more question, sir. Could you tell me about the religious instruction of children?"

"That duty is performed for us by the robot-confessors."

"Yes?"

"The notion came to us from the ancient root-faith of Transcendental Freudianism. The robot-confessor instructs children and adults alike. It hears their problems within the social matrix. It is their constant friend, their social mentor, their religious instructor. Being robotic, the confessors are able to give exact and unvarying answers to any question. This aids the great work of Conformity."

"I can see that it does. What do the human priests do?"

"They watch over the robot-confessors."

"Are these robot-confessors present in the closed classrooms?"

"I am not competent to answer that."

"They are, aren't they?"

"I truly do not know. The closed classrooms are closed to abbots as well as other adults."

"By whose order?"

"By order of the Chief of the Secret Police."

"I see... Thank you, Citizen Abbot Boeren."

(Citizen Enyen Dravivian, age 43, occupation government employee. A narrow-faced, slit-eyed man, old and tired beyond his years.)

"Good afternoon, sir. You say that you are employed by the government?"

"Correct."

"Is that the state or the federal government?"

"Both."

"I see. And have you been in this employ for very long?"

"Approximately eighteen years."

"Yes, sir. Would you mind telling me what, specifically, your job is?"

"Not at all. I am the Chief of the Secret Police."

"You are—I see, sir. That's very interesting. I—"

"Don't reach for your needlebeam, ex-Citizen Barrent. I can assure you, it won't operate in the blanketed area around this house. And if you draw it, you'll be hurt."

"How?"

"I have my own means of protection."

"How did you know my name?"

"I've known about you almost since you set foot upon Earth. We are not entirely without resources you know. But we can discuss all that inside. Won't you come in?"

"I think I'd rather not."

"I'm afraid you have to. Come, Barrent, I won't bite you."

"Am I under arrest?"

"Of course not. We're simply going to have a little talk. That's right, sir, right through there. Just make yourself comfortable."

CHAPTER TWENTY-EIGHT

Dravivian led him into a large room paneled in walnut. The furniture was of a heavy, black wood, intricately carved and varnished. The desk, high and straight, seemed to be an antique. A heavy tapestry covered one entire wall. It depicted, in fading colors, a medieval hunting scene.

"Do you like it?" Dravivian asked. "My family did the furnishing. My wife copied the tapestry from an original in the Metropolitan Museum. My two sons collaborated on the furniture. They wanted something ancient and Spanish in feeling, but with more comfort than antiques usually give. A slight modification of the lines accomplished that. My own contributions are not visible. Music of the baroque period is my specialty."

"Aside from policework," Barrent said.

"Yes, aside from that." Dravivian turned away from Barrent and looked thoughtfully at the tapestry. "We will come to the matter of the police in due course. Tell me first, what do you think of this room?"

"It's very beautiful," Barrent said.

"Yes. And?"

"Well—I'm no judge."

"You *must* judge," Dravivian said. "In this room you can see Earth's civilization in miniature. Tell me what you think of it."

"It feels lifeless," Barrent said.

Dravivian turned to Barrent and smiled. "Yes, that's a good word for it. Self-involved might perhaps be better. This is a high-status room, Barrent. A great deal of creativity has gone into the artistic improvement of ancient archetypes. My family has re-created a bit of the Spanish past, as others have re-created bits of the Mayan, Early American, or Oceanic past. And yet, the essential hollowness is obvious. Our automatized factories produce the same goods for us year in and year out. Since everyone has these same goods, it is necessary for us to change the factory product, to improve and embroider it, to express ourselves through it, to rank ourselves by it. That's how Earth is, Barrent. Our energy and skills are channeled into essentially decadent pursuits. We re-carve old furniture, worry about rank and status, and in the meantime the frontier of the distant planets remains unexplored and unconquered. We ceased long ago to expand. Stability brought the danger of stagnation, to which we succumbed. We became so highly socialized that individuality had to be diverted to the most harmless of pursuits, turned inward, kept from any meaningful expression. I think you have seen a fair amount of that in your time on Earth?"

"I have. But I never expected to hear the Chief of the Secret Police say it."

"I'm an unusual man," Dravivian said, with a mocking smile. "And the Secret Police is an unusual institution."

"It must be very efficient. How did you find out about me?"

"That was really quite simple. Most of the people of Earth are security-conditioned from childhood. It's part of our heritage, you know. Nearly all the people you met were able to tell that there was something very wrong about you. You were as obviously out of place as a wolf among sheep. People noticed, and reported directly to me."

"All right," Barrent said. "Now what?"

"First I would like you to tell me about Omega."

Barrent told the Police Chief about his life on the prison planet. Dravivian nodded, a faint smile on his lips.

"Yes, it's very much as I expected," he said. "The same sort of thing has happened on Omega as happened in early America and Australia. There are differences, of course; you have been shut off more completely from the mother country. But the same fierce energy and drive is there, and the same ruthlessness."

"What are you going to do?" Barrent asked.

Dravivian shrugged his shoulders. "It really doesn't matter. I suppose I could kill you. But that wouldn't stop your group on Omega from sending out other spies, or from seizing one of the prison ships. As soon as the Omegans begin to move in force, they'll discover the truth anyhow."

"What truth?"

"By now it must be obvious to you," Dravivian said. "Earth hasn't fought a war for nearly eight hundred years. We wouldn't know how. The organization of guardships around Omega is pure façade. The ships are completely automatized, built to meet conditions of several hundreds years ago. A determined attack will capture a ship; and when you have one, the rest will fall. After that, there's nothing to stop the Omegans from coming back to Earth; and there's nothing on Earth to fight them with. This is the reason why all prisoners leaving Earth are divorced from their memories. If they *remembered*, Earth's vulnerability would be painfully apparent."

"If you knew all this," Barrent asked, "why didn't your leaders do something about it?"

"That was our original intention. But there was no real drive behind the intention. We preferred not to think about it. We assumed the status quo would remain indefinitely. We didn't want to think about the day when the Omegans returned to Earth."

"What are you and your police going to do about it?" Barrent asked.

"I am façade, too," Dravivian told him. "I have no police. The position of Chief is entirely honorary. There has been no need of a police force on Earth for close to a century."

"You're going to need one when the Omegans come home," Barrent said.

"Yes. There's going to be crime again, and serious trouble. But I think the final amalgamation will be successful. You on Omega have the drive, the ambition to reach the stars. I believe you need a certain stability and creativeness which Earth can provide. Whatever the results, the union is inevitable. We've lived in a dream here for too long. It's going to take violent measures to awaken us."

Dravivian rose to his feet. "And now," he said, "since the fate of Earth and Omega seem to be decided, could I offer you some refreshment?"

CHAPTER TWENTY-NINE

With the help of the Chief of Police, Barrent put a message aboard the next ship to leave for Omega. The message told about conditions on Earth and urged immediate action. When that was finished, Barrent was ready for his final job—to find the judge who had sentenced him for a crime he hadn't committed, and the lying informer who had turned him in to the judge. When he found those two, Barrent knew he would regain the missing portions of his memory.

He took the night expressway to Youngerstun. His suspicions, sharply keyed from life on Omega, would not let him rest. There had to be a catch to all this splendid simplicity. Perhaps he would find it in Youngerstun.

By early morning he was there. Superficially, the neat rows of houses looked the same as in any other town. But for Barrent they were different, and achingly familiar. He *remembered* this town, and the monotonous houses had individuality and meaning for him. He had been born and raised in this town.

There was Grothmeir's store, and across the street was the home of Havening, the local interior decorating champion. Here was Billy Havelock's house. Billy had been his best friend. They had planned on being starmen together, and had remained good friends after school—until Barrent had been sentenced to Omega.

Here was Andrew Therkaler's house. And down the block was the school he had attended. He could remember the classes. He could remember how, every day, they had gone through the door that led to the closed class. But he still could not remember what he had learned there.

Right here, near two huge elms, the murder had taken place. Barrent walked to the spot and remembered how it had happened. He had been on his way home. From somewhere down the street he had heard a scream. He had turned, and a man—Illiardi—had run down the street and thrown something at him. Barrent had caught it instinctively and found himself holding an illegal handgun. A few steps further, he had looked into the twisted dead face of Andrew Therkaler.

And what had happened next? Confusion. Panic. A sensation of someone watching as he stood, weapon in hand, over the corpse. There, at the end of the street, was the refuge to which he had gone.

He walked up to it, and recognized it as a robot-confessional booth.

Barrent entered the booth. It was small, and there was a faint odor of incense in the air. The room contained a single chair. Facing it was a complex, brilliantly lighted panel.

"Good morning, Will," the panel said to him.

Barrent had a sudden sense of helplessness when he heard that soft mechanical voice. He remembered it now. The passionless voice knew all, understood all, and forgave nothing. That artfully manufactured voice had spoken to him, had listened, and then had judged. In his dream, he had personified the robot-confessor into the figure of a human judge.

"You remember me?" Barrent asked.

"Of course," said the robot-confessor. "You were one of my parishioners before you went to Omega."

"You sent me there."

"For the crime of murder."

"But I didn't commit the crime!" Barrent said. "I didn't do it, and you must have known it!"

"Of course I knew it," the robot-confessor said. "But my powers and duties are strictly defined. I sentence according to evidence, not intuition. By law, the robot-confessors must weigh only the concrete evidence which is put before them. They must, when in doubt, sentence. In fact, the mere presence of a man before me charged with murder must be taken as a strong presumption of his guilt."

"Was there evidence against me?"

"Yes."

"Who gave it?"

"I cannot reveal his name."

"You must!" Barrent said. "Times are changing on Earth. The prisoners are coming back. Did you know that?"

"I expected it," the robot-confessor said.

"I must have the informer's name," Barrent said. He took the needlebeam out of his pocket and advanced toward the panel.

"A machine cannot be coerced," the robot-confessor told him.

"Give me the name!" Barrent shouted.

"I should not, for your own good. The danger would be too great. Believe me, Will..."

"The name!"

"Very well. You will find the informer at Thirty-five Maple Street. But I earnestly advise you not to go there. You will be killed. You simply do not know—"

Barrent pressed the trigger, and the narrow beam scythed through the panel. Lights flashed and faded as he cut through the intricate wiring. At last all the lights were dead, and a faint gray smoke came from the panel.

Barrent left the booth. He put the needlebeam back in his pocket and walked to Maple Street.

He had been here before. He knew this street, set upon a hill, rising steeply between oak and maple trees. Those lampposts were old friends, that crack in the pavement was an ancient landmark. Here were the houses, heavy with familiarity. They seemed to lean expectantly toward him, like spectators waiting for the final act of an almost forgotten drama.

He stood in front of 35 Maple Street. The silence which surrounded that plain white-shuttered house struck him as ominous. He took the needlebeam out of his pocket, looking for a reassurance he knew he could not find. Then he walked up the neat flagstones and tried the front door. It opened. He stepped inside.

He made out the dim shades of lamps and furniture, the dull gleam of a painting on the wall, a piece of statuary on an ebony pedestal. Needlebeam in hand, he stepped into the next room.

And came face to face with the informer.

Staring at the informer's face, Barrent remembered. In an overpowering flood of memory he saw himself, a little boy, entering the closed classroom. He heard again the soothing hum of machinery, watched the pretty lights blink and flash, heard the insinuating machine voice whisper in his ear. At first, the voice filled him with horror; what it suggested was unthinkable. Then, slowly, he became accustomed to it, and accustomed to all the strange things that happened in the closed classroom.

He *learned.* The machines taught on deep, unconscious levels. The machines intertwined their lessons with the basic drives, weaving a pattern of learned behavior with the life instinct. They taught, then blocked off conscious knowledge of the lessons, sealed it—and fused it.

What had he been taught? *For the social good, you must be your own policeman and witness. You must assume responsibility for any crime which might conceivably be yours.*

The face of the informer stared impassively at him. It was Barrent's own face, reflected back from a mirror on the wall.

He had informed on himself. Standing with the gun in his hand that day, looking down at the murdered man, learned unconscious processes had taken over. The presumption of guilt had been too great for him to resist, the similarity to guilt had turned into guilt itself. He had walked to the robot-confessor's booth, and there he had given complete and damning evidence against himself, had indicted himself on the basis of probability.

The robot-confessor had passed the obligatory sentence and Barrent had left the booth. Well-trained in the lessons of the classroom, he had taken himself into custody, had gone to the nearest thought-control center in Trenton. Already a partial amnesia had taken place, keyed to and triggered by the lessons of the closed classroom.

The skilled android technicians in the thought-control center had labored hard to complete this amnesia, to obliterate any remnants of memory. As a standard safeguard against any possible recovering of his memory, they had implanted a logical construct of his crime beneath the conscious level. As the regulations required, this construct contained an implication of the far-reaching power of Earth.

When the job was completed, an automatized Barrent had marched out of the center, taken a special expressway to the prison ship depot, boarded the prison ship, entered his cell, and closed the door and left Earth behind him. Then he had slept until the checkpoint had been passed, after which the newly arrived guards awakened the prisoners for disembarkation on Omega...

Now, staring at his own face in the mirror, the last of the conscious lessons of the classroom became conscious:

The lessons of the closed classroom must never be consciously known by the individual. If they become conscious the human organism must perform an immediate act of self-destruction.

Now he saw why his conquest of Earth had been so easy; it was because he had conquered nothing. Earth needed no security forces, for the policeman and the executioner were implanted in every man's mind. Beneath the surface of Earth's mild and pleasant culture was a self-perpetuating robot civilization. An awareness of that civilization was punishable by death.

And here, at this moment, the real struggle for Earth began.

Learned behavior patterns intertwined with basic life drives forced Barrent to raise the needlebeam, to point it toward his head. This was what the robot-confessor had tried to warn him about, and what the mutant girl had skrenned. The younger Barrent, conditioned to absolute and mindless conformity, had to kill himself.

The older Barrent who had spent time on Omega fought that blind urge. A schizophrenic Barrent fought himself. The two parts of him battled for possession of the weapon, for control of the body, for ownership of the mind.

The needlebeam's movement stopped inches from his head. The muzzle wavered. Then slowly, the new Omegan Barrent, Barrent$_2$, forced the weapon away.

His victory was short-lived. For now the lessons of the closed classroom took over, forcing Barrent$_2$ into a contrasurvival struggle with the implacable and death-desiring Barrent$_1$.

CHAPTER THIRTY

Conditioning took over and flung the fighting Barrents backward through subjective time, to those stress points in the past where death had been near, where the temporal life fabric had been weakened, where a predisposition toward death had already been established. Conditioning forced Barrent$_2$ to re-experience those moments. But this time, the danger was augmented by the full force of the malignant half of his personality—by the murderous informer, Barrent$_1$.

Barrent$_2$ stood under glaring lights on the blood-stained sands of the Arena, a sword in his hand. It was the time of the Omegan Games. Coming at him was the Saunus, a heavily armored reptile with the leering face of Barrent$_1$. Barrent$_2$ severed the creature's tail, and it changed into three trichomotreds, rat-sized, Barrent-faced, with the dispositions of rabid wolverines. He killed two, and the third grinned and bit his left hand to the bone. He killed it, and watched Barrent$_1$'s blood leak into the soggy sand...

THREE RAGGED men sat laughing on a bench, and a girl handed him a small gun. "Luck," she said. "I hope you know how to use this." Barrent nodded his thanks before he noticed that the girl was not Moera; she was the skrenning mutant who had predicted his death. Still, he moved into the street and faced the three Hadjis.

Two of the men were mild-faced strangers. The third, Barrent$_1$, stepped forward and quickly brought his gun into firing position. Barrent$_2$ flung himself to the ground and pressed the trigger of his unfamiliar weapon. He felt it vibrate in his hand and saw Hadji Barrent's head and shoulders turn black and begin to crumble. Before he could take aim again, his gun was wrenched violently from his hand. Barrent₁'s dying shot had creased the end of the muzzle.

Desperately he dived for the weapon, and as he rolled toward it he saw the second man, now wearing the Barrent₁ face, take careful aim. Barrent₂ felt pain flash through his arm, already torn by the trichomotred's teeth. He managed to shoot this Barrent₁, and through a haze of pain faced the third man, now also Barrent₁. His arm was stiffening rapidly, but he forced himself to press the trigger...

You're playing their game, Barrent₂ told himself. The death-conditioning will wear you down, will kill you. *You must see through it, get past it. It isn't really happening, it's in your mind...*

But there was no time to think. He was in a large, circular, high-ceilinged room of stone in the cellars of the Department of Justice. It was the Trial by Ordeal. Rolling across the floor toward him was a glistening black machine shaped like a half-sphere, standing almost four feet high. It came at him, and in the pattern of red, green, and amber lights he could see the hated face of Barrent₁.

Now his enemy was in its ultimate form: the invariant robot consciousness, as false and stylized as the conditioned dreams of Earth. The Barrent₁ machine extruded a single slender tentacle with a white light winking at the end of it. As it approached, the tentacle withdrew, and in its place appeared a jointed metal arm ending in a knife-edge. Barrent₂ dodged, and heard the knife scrape against the stone.

It isn't what you think it is, Barrent₂ told himself. *It isn't a machine, and you are not back on Omega. This is only half of yourself you are fighting, this is nothing but a deadly illusion.*

But he couldn't believe it. The Barrent machine was coming at him again, its metal hide glistening with a foul green substance which Barrent₂ recognized immediately as Contact Poison. He broke into a sprint, trying to stay away from the fatal touch.

It isn't fatal, he told himself.

Neutralizer washed over the metal surface, clearing away the poison. The machine tried to ram him. Barrent tried half-heartedly to push it aside. It crashed into him with stunning force, and he could feel ribs splintering.

It isn't real! You're letting a conditioned reflex talk you to death! You aren't on Omega, but on Earth, in your own home, staring into a mirror!

But the pain was real, and the clubbed metal arm felt real as it crashed against his shoulder. Barrent staggered away.

He felt horror, not at dying, but at dying too soon, before he could warn the Omegans of this ultimate danger planted deep in their minds. There was no one else to warn of the disaster that would strike each man as he recovered his specific memories of Earth. To his best knowledge, no one had experienced this and lived. If *he* could live through it, countermeasures could be taken, counter-conditioning could be set up.

He pulled himself to his feet. Coached since childhood in social responsibility, he thought of it now. He couldn't allow himself to die when his knowledge was vital to Omega.

This is not a real machine.

He repeated it to himself as the Barrent machine revved up, picked up speed, and hurtled toward him from the far side of the room. He forced himself to see beyond the machine, to see the patient droning lessons of the classroom which had created this monster in his mind.

This is not a real machine.

He believed it…

And swung his fist into the hated face reflected in the metal.

There was a moment of dazzling pain, and then he lost consciousness. When he came to, he was alone in his own home on Earth. His arm and shoulder ached, and several of his ribs seemed to be broken. On his left hand he bore the stigmata of the trichomotred's bite.

But with his cut and bleeding right hand he had smashed the mirror. He had shattered it and Barrent₁ utterly and forever.

THE END

If you've enjoyed this book, you will not want to miss these terrific titles…

ARMCHAIR SCI-FI, FANTASY, & HORROR DOUBLE NOVELS, $12.95 each

D-81 **THE LAST PLEA** by Robert Bloch
OMEGA by Robert Sheckley

D-82 **WOMAN FROM ANOTHER PLANET** by Frank Belknap Long
HOMECALLING by Judith Merril

D-83 **WHEN TWO WORLDS MEET** by Robert Moore Williams
THE MAN WHO HAD NO BRAINS by Jeff Sutton

D-84 **THE SPECTRE OF SUICIDE SWAMP** by E. K. Jarvis
IT'S MAGIC, YOU DOPE! by Jack Sharkey

D-85 **THE STARSHIP FROM SIRIUS** by Rog Phillips
FINAL WEAPON by Everett Cole

D-86 **TREASURE ON THUNDER MOON** by Edmond Hamilton
TRAIL OF THE ASTROGAR by Henry Haase

D-87 **VENGEANCE OF KYVOR** by Randall Garrett
AT THE EARTH'S CORE by Edgar Rice Burroughs

D-88 **THE MAD ROBOT** by William P. McGivern
THE RUNNING MAN by J. Holly Hunter

D-89 **THE WOMAN IN SKIN 13** by Paul W. Fairman
THE VENUS ENIGMA by Joe Gibson

D-90 **DWELLERS OF THE DEEP** by Don Wilcox
NIGHT OF THE LONG KNIVES by Fritz Leiber

ARMCHAIR SCIENCE FICTION CLASSICS, $12.95 each

C-28 **THE MAN FROM TOMORROW**
by Stanton A. Cobllentz

C-29 **THE GREEN MAN OF GRAYPEC**
by Festus Pragnell

C-30 **THE SHAVER MYSTERY, Book Four**
by Richard S. Shaver

ARMCHAIR MASTERS OF SCIENCE FICTION SERIES, $16.95 each

MS-7 **MASTERS OF SCIENCE FICTION AND FANTASY, Vol. Seven**
Lester del Rey, "The Band Played On" and other tales

MS-8 **MASTERS OF SCIENCE FICTION, Vol. Eight**
Milton Lesser, "'A' is for Android" and other tales

www.ingramcontent.com/pod-product-compliance
Lightning Source LLC
Chambersburg PA
CBHW030309180626
46810CB00003B/988